Readers love
M.J. O'SHEA

Soufflés at Sunrise

"Like a nice warm blanket; it keeps you cozy, makes you want to snuggle and just feels damn good."

—MM Good Book Reviews

"If you are looking for a well-written, entertaining and very sexy story, then *Soufflés at Sunrise* is definitely for you. It is just what this reader needed to keep me warm on a very cold winter's night."

—Top 2 Bottom Reviews

Corkscrewed

"I've read four or five books by M.J. now, and I've enjoyed all of them. She writes good character driven stories, with great plots. This is another great book from her!"

—Love Bytes

"So I pretty much loved this entire story… Unique. Likable characters. Great chemistry between the MCs. Fun! Another really good book by this author."

—It's About The Book

The Luckiest (with Piper Vaughn)

"I loved this book the first time 'round and if possible I loved it even more the second time round."

—Prism Book Alliance

"Definitely recommend this to everyone."

—The Novel Approach

By M.J. O'SHEA

Catch My Breath
Cross Bones (Dreamspinner Anthology)
Corkscrewed
Family Jewels
Newton's Laws of Attraction • Impractical Magic
Stroke!

ROCK BAY
Coming Home
Letting Go
Finding Shelter

With Anna Martin
JUST DESSERTS
Macarons at Midnight
Soufflés at Sunrise

With Piper Vaughn
LUCKY MOON
Moonlight Becomes You
The Luckiest

ONE THING
One Small Thing
One True Thing

Published by DREAMSPINNER PRESS
http://www.dreamspinnerpress.com

FAMILY JEWELS

M.J. O'SHEA

DREAMSPINNER PRESS

Published by
DREAMSPINNER PRESS

5032 Capital Circle SW, Suite 2, PMB# 279, Tallahassee, FL 32305-7886 USA
http://www.dreamspinnerpress.com/

Family Jewels
© 2015 M.J. O'Shea.

Cover Art
© 2015 L.C. Chase.
http://www.lcchase.com
Cover content is for illustrative purposes only and any person depicted on the cover is a model.

ISBN: 978-1-63476-073-7
Digital ISBN: 978-1-63476-074-4
Library of Congress Control Number: 2014922886
First Edition April 2015

Printed in the United States of America
(∞)
This paper meets the requirements of
ANSI/NISO Z39.48-1992 (Permanence of Paper).

Thank you to Ari for being a great cheerleader! I couldn't have done it without you. :) xoxo
    —MJ

CHAPTER ONE

London
March

"WE'VE GOT something you need to see, Luke. You'd better get over here now."

Luke Eldridge sighed into his phone. He glanced at the slices of pizza he'd just picked up from a food cart down on Camden Lock. Looked like there was more cold pizza in his future. Typical. Irritating, but typical.

"Where are you?" Luke asked. He dragged himself off his soft leather couch. It made a disgusting squelching sound. Luke turned and halfheartedly wiped the seat off. He was tired from the run he'd forced himself to take, wet, and starting to chill as heat escaped through his damp T-shirt. The last thing he wanted to do was get back into a suit and go out in the cold he'd just escaped from.

Rob, one of his oldest friends from his days in the FBI academy, who'd followed Luke when he transferred to London, rattled off a very upper crust Kensington address.

"Jesus. Is this one going to make the morning press?" Luke asked. People who lived at addresses like that tended to make the news. His job was always harder when he had a ton of panicking socialites breathing down his neck, guarding their remaining beloved possessions. He didn't need them or the news vans hovering outside his crime scene.

"Probably. I'll try to put it off as long as I can, but you know how it works. Just get your ass over here. Waterman's on my dick already."

"Sounds unpleasant." Luke chuckled under his breath. "Does that surprise you?"

"Not really."

Didn't surprise Luke either. George Waterman, their division chief within Interpol Art Crimes, was all about the high profile cases. Art, jewelry, anyone with a Lord or Lady attached to the front of their name. Even the odd Sir here and there. Cases like that were good press for the agency, he always said. Probably more like good for getting his face on the camera. Waterman was a media whore extraordinaire. Usually Luke didn't care, but when they were in the middle of trying to open a case, it kind of pissed him off.

Luke felt it would be better to deal with the press *after* they had some solid leads, or, you know, someone in custody, but far be it from him to correct Waterman. He'd spent the last eight years trying to overcome the hereditary American-ness Waterman deemed a deep character flaw. If he started correcting the guy now, he might as well sign his own pink slip.

"I can be there in fifteen minutes. Waterman won't even be done fixing his hair for the cameras," Luke told Rob. He was already in his suit pants and shaking out his dress shirt. It felt a little stale from a long day, but he wasn't going to put on a new one for a late evening call. If all went well, Luke would be back in his sweats and on his couch in less than an hour.

"Try to make it ten. I'm not in the mood to get my skin pulled off a strip at a time."

He sounded like his typical sarcastic self, but the tone of his friend's voice was different. Worried, maybe. Luke knew that tone. It rarely led to good news. "What's going on, Rob? What are you leaving out?"

"There's something weird about this one. Might cause us a hell of a shit storm in the near future if I'm right."

"Are you going to tell me or are we going to play guessing games?" Luke wasn't in the mood to play anything. All he wanted to do was eat some still-warm pizza, crawl into bed, and sleep for days—or at least until his alarm went off at six. He'd gotten way too little sleep lately. He hadn't gotten enough sleep in years.

Rob cleared his throat nervously. "You need to see this for yourself. Just get here, man."

Luke disconnected the call. He finished dressing, shoved one piece of his pizza onto a paper towel, and grabbed his keys. He could eat it on the way without ruining his suit. Even if he spilled, fuck it. He wasn't going to sacrifice one more decent dinner to the cause.

THE LONDON streets were slick and dark, half frozen in the early spring chill, but at least it was quiet. The air was close to freezing, too. Unseasonably low temps, but sadly not by much. After all the years he'd been in London, the winters still got to him, cold and wet, the kind that seemed to creep all the way into the center of his chest—nothing like his childhood home in South Carolina or even Virginia, where he'd lived and worked his first few years out of the academy. Sometimes Luke missed the old optimistic years at Quantico. These days it seemed like the cold was impossible to shake. It seeped into his bones and camped out until nothing he did could warm him through.

Fuck, I'm getting old.

The stone row houses slipped past, nestled together, dark on the outside like everything else, interiors shining and cheery against the insidious, creeping chill. Everyone who knew better was inside somewhere, enjoying dinner, relaxing with the people they loved. They weren't alone. He'd figured long ago his hopes for being one of them had probably passed. Luke loved his job, it was his life, but some nights he wouldn't mind a break. Luke bypassed their unit's Westminster offices in favor of going straight to the scene. He didn't need anything but what he had on him. Hopefully he'd be in and out in time for the late news.

PARKING WAS typically a nightmare in residential areas of London, especially with most people home out of the rain, but he maneuvered his way into a spot only a block and a half away from his destination and called it a miracle.

It was easy to tell which house was the target. The small drive was crammed full of official-looking vehicles, lit brightly, and festooned with crime scene tape. His unit had made quick progress of blocking it off. Scotland Yard was there too. Leland Chapman, one of the detectives Luke had had a few unpleasant run-ins with, was standing out front with Rob, probably getting into it with him over jurisdiction, a routine yet annoying squabble. Luke walked a little faster so he could rescue Rob. Rob didn't deserve to get his blood pressure up over nothing. The beef really was between Chapman and him. They'd rubbed each other the wrong way since day one.

"Leland," Luke murmured when he got there. The tension was thick, and Rob's face had turned a bit red in the cold. Yep. They'd been arguing.

"I'm glad you're here," Rob said pointedly. "Get up here before Leland fucks up the scene."

"I know how to do my job. This is my city," Leland said.

"Interpol's been on this case for years. Call your director if you want. He'll fill you in. This is ours." Rob dismissed Leland and turned for the white stairs into the townhouse.

"Were you blowing smoke up his ass?" Luke asked quietly. How the hell could Rob know who had rights to the case? It was only a few hours old.

"Nope. We were flagged right away. Come upstairs and you'll see why soon enough."

The outside of the place was imposing, tall, and narrow, pristine even in the wet, cold dark. Luke trailed Rob up the slick stairs, more than a little curious about what had his oldest friend acting so strangely.

"Remember our training at the academy?" Rob asked.

Why's he bringing that up? Luke didn't think Rob could read his mind, know that he'd been thinking about the good old days earlier—times when he thought in black and white and everything seemed so obvious.

"Of course. I'm thirty-eight, not a hundred."

"Right, old man. You're getting a little fuzzy around the edges."

Luke elbowed him. "You're six months older than me."

Rob smiled and gestured for Luke to follow him into the house. They wound their way through an opulent but cramped hallway, up two flights of stairs carpeted with Persian runners and flanked by creepy portraits that leered at him in the dark. The stairs seemed never-ending after a long day and an even longer run, but Luke trudged on. Finally they stopped on the third floor and turned into what must've been a master suite. At first glance it looked like nothing was out of place: the bed neatly made, carpets vacuumed to perfection, lamp on and glowing against taupe and silver damask wallpaper. But then Luke looked into the en suite bathroom and saw it. Inside a gold-leafed wardrobe was a small safe, cracked open and yawning empty except for two very, *very* noticeable details.

No fucking way.

Hanging over the door of the safe, glinting dully in the lamplight, was an antique pocket watch. Underneath it, stark white on the carpeting, was a scrap of paper barely big enough for the six typed lines on it.

Wind moves harsh on Autumn wings
Blue as heart and flowers to the stone
Rend love from love
and ash from earth
'Til God's seed is shriveled and spent
Empty and wasted with regret

"That's Ezra Covington. Nineteenth-century American poet. I'll be shocked if it's not." Luke didn't have to look it up. He didn't know the poem but knew the pattern of what they'd found better than he knew his parents' faces. A cleaned-out safe, an old watch, and a Covington poem on a scrap of linen paper, typed out on an antique Underwood typewriter, just like always. But it *couldn't* be. Not after so much time.

Rob nodded. "Yeah, we had Morgan do a search for that verse as soon as we got to the scene to confirm. It's a Covington poem. You thinking what I'm thinking?"

"*Fuck*," Luke whispered.

"Yup, that's pretty much what I'm thinking." Rob looked equal parts amused and concerned. "Could it be him?"

Luke sure as hell knew why Rob had taken a momentary stroll down memory lane. He remembered every detail they'd learned, down to the color of the rugs in the crime scene photos—missing jewelry, art, antiques, never found, nobody caught. The only things that linked the crimes were the damn antique pocket watches and the thief's weakness for Covington's poetry.

They'd studied it for weeks back at the academy, even though the FBI hadn't been involved in every aspect of the case like Interpol had. It was the reason he and Rob had gotten so close. They'd shared an interest in the old case. Expensive, sometimes priceless jewelry, art, artifacts stolen from high-risk locations and the location marked every single time with two things: a verse of poetry and an antique watch. Rob and Luke had pored over the pictures and reports as trainees, hours and hours of theory and discussion. It had been an obsession back then. He'd shoved it away, figured it was impossible to solve a case so cold.

"I can't believe it," Luke said. "It just... no. Agility alone would rule him out. And he's been inactive for so long. Why start again now?" Luke pressed fingers into his eye sockets and rubbed. He tried to make sense of what was a very clear crime scene with a huge red arrow pointing with flashing lights in one direction only.

The Nightwatchman.

IT WAS goddamn impossible, is what it was. The Nightwatchman had already been gone a few years when Luke had studied him at the academy. Luke did some mental calculations. Twenty years. It had been a little over twenty years since he'd surfaced. The FBI and Interpol and always assumed it was a man. He'd have to be in his late fifties at least if their old profile had been correct. Luke tried to wrap his head around it.

"You think we have a copycat?" Rob asked.

Luke was still trying to process the perfect details on the scene, the sheer improbability of what he was looking at. The thought of original versus copycat was about sixty steps ahead of where he was. "I don't know, man."

"But I thought the full details were never released to the public. The watches, yes. After all, it was the press who dubbed him. But the Covington poems? Nobody should know that part."

Luke turned, surprised to hear another voice in the room. "Thanks, Kelly."

He'd been so shell-shocked by the watch and the poem, he'd barely noticed her walk into the room. She was fresh on the case, didn't have the extensive background that he and Rob had. It might end up being an advantage. Less preconceptions. Still, the Nightwatchman case was legend. "If we have a copycat here, they have insider knowledge somehow."

"Let's get Scotland Yard back in here to process the scene," Luke said. "I need time to think."

HE'D ALWAYS felt like a spider, scuttling through the underbelly of the city, unseen until he was nearly gone, an oily black streak in the corner of people's vision. He was meant for the dark corners. Meant for the night.

Corbin Ford had had a long life of skating along unnoticed by most. It should've been something that bothered him. It would bother most people. But he liked it. Liked that the woman who might smile condescendingly at him at the bank, then forget he ever existed, could be the same one he divested of everything of value hours later. It felt like an inside joke, one he never planned to share with anyone. He belonged on the outside looking in. He was comfortable there, had been for thirty-five years.

He was a shadow, and like one, he moved silently through the city.

A taxi drove past and sent up a huge spray of water. He managed to jump out of the way of the plume fast enough he barely got any on his coat. He'd paid enough for the damn thing. It'd be annoying to get it ruined. Sure, he could afford to replace the coat and buy hundreds more just like it, but it didn't mean he wanted to.

Corbin swore under his breath and moved closer to the buildings.

It was still damn cold for March. Damn cold period as far as he was concerned. He tightened his jacket against the bitter chill and wrapped his black scarf tighter around his neck. Black jacket, black scarf, dark jeans, and black shoes. He fit in in the city. Nobody would notice anything unusual about him.

Corbin knew he shouldn't have been there, so close to the scene. It was stupid to stay and watch the house swarm with police and agents, but he'd needed more satisfaction somehow. The clink of Lady Dalton's emerald earrings and the thick, heavy ruby-and-diamond necklace weren't enough for him anymore. He'd spent nearly an hour with the jewels earlier, trying to get the same feeling he used to get from a particularly good haul. He'd touched the gems and weighed them in his hand. Even when he'd put them away in a safe far better than the one he'd fished them out of, there was barely a spark. No heavy dark thrill. No excitement. The rest of her things weren't worth more than a moment's examination. He'd stolen them for the resale cash, not any particular pleasure. The emeralds were different. So was that necklace. At least it would've been in the past.

Corbin felt like he was broken.

In retrospect, that was probably why he'd done it. Why he'd left the watch and the poem for the authorities to find. Interpol was there; they had to be. He hadn't seen them, but leaving his father's old trademark was a sure bet to get them called. No more was Corbin "a rash of high-end burglaries." No. He'd just become a singular and quite important someone. A thief who was supposedly long gone.

A legend.

The little missing thrill, the one he'd tried desperately to get from cold jewels and heavy gold, wound its way up his back when he thought about the Interpol agents finding his adopted calling card. He smiled into the dark.

Corbin's phone rang. He checked the caller ID with a groan. Wouldn't do any good to ignore her. It never worked. He impatiently swiped a freezing finger across the screen.

"Mom. How's the weather in Palm Beach?" he asked. He waited for the hammer of her anger to drop hard and heavy right on his head.

"Corbin, what have you done?" she hissed. "Are you out of your goddamn mind?"

His mother rarely disappointed. It was hard not to laugh. Just that much made the excitement he'd been missing thrum through his veins once again. He never would've thought he'd need the recognition; he'd always said the jewels, the paintings, the rare books were the only things that made his heart pitter-patter. He guessed he didn't know himself as well as he thought.

"I see news travels fast. Did you two hire a new guy to hack into Interpol's system? You know you can just text me if you want to know what I'm up to. I will answer if I'm not too busy." He flicked his hair out of his face. "That way you won't be responsible for someone else's arrest. You know I hate when we rope other people into our family squabbles."

Corbin knew exactly how to pull every one of his mother's strings. Her vast annoyance radiated the entire way across the Atlantic. Corbin didn't know why it was so fun to antagonize her. He loved his mom to death, but still he grinned into his phone.

"Why did you stir up a hornet's nest that's been buried for years?" His mother was trying to control her considerable temper. He hadn't had so much fun in months, if not far longer. It was way past time.

"I was bored?" He shrugged. "It wasn't exciting anymore."

"I think you need to come home. Steal a few paintings from some galleries in town. Cool your heels. I'm working on a four-man job in Beverly Hills that I think you—"

"Florida's not home for me, Mom. And I'm not moving to California. Ever. I think I'm liking it here. The rain's growing on me." He'd landed in London a few months before, got his bearings, found a place to live, then got to work. It took planning to do what he did. Preparation. He was damn good at it, but it was still complicated.

His mother made a strangled noise on the other side of the line. "I could have Jeremy sic Interpol on you. Make you run so fast you won't have time for any more ridiculous stunts."

Corbin let himself laugh out loud. "You could, but you won't. Tell Jeremy hello for me. I think I'm still a few points ahead. Especially after tonight. That was definitely a level up. He'd better do something big if he doesn't want me to leave him in the dust."

They were both good thieves—they'd learned from the best, after all—but Corbin was just the tiniest bit smarter than his older brother. He liked to lord it over him from time to time, just like Jeremy rarely lost an opportunity to point out that he was their father's favorite son. It was dysfunctional as hell, but it was their relationship, and they both loved it the way it was.

"You need to get out of there before you get caught." His mother was nothing if not repetitive if there was something she really wanted him to get into his thick skull. And Corbin was about as interested in listening as usual.

"I'll leave like I always do… when I'm tired of this scene." Corbin looked around at the gloom and rain and slick, dark stone. He'd get tired of it eventually. London was exciting, but the weather sucked. He sensed palm trees somewhere in his future. Cannes maybe. Rio. Somewhere sunny with miles of beach and even more careless rich people for him to play with. "And I won't get caught. I never do. I'm going to stop for some dinner, Ma. I like the curry here. Have a good day, and give Dad a hug for me."

"Your fa—"

Corbin hung up before his mother could tell him exactly what his father thought of him abruptly deciding to fill his very large and famous shoes. Corbin had been stealing for years, nothing that could be linked to a single person. He didn't even stick to a single type of haul, though the shine of stones always made him the most happy. Corbin was tired of floating beneath the radar. He hadn't been lying. It had gotten boring. He had plenty of money, enough that he could've done what his father had at his age—retire to a beach house and grow organic oranges. That life wasn't for him. Corbin thought he had too much of his mother in his blood. She'd never be done, and neither would he.

THE GAME was about to begin, and he couldn't wait.

CHAPTER TWO

"HEY, YOU want to come over for dinner? Trish made your favorite." Rob nudged Luke's shoulder as they walked out of the most puzzling crime scene of their considerable careers and back into the freezing rain.

He had that pizza at home, but it was likely cold and congealed on his counter. He'd never been a fan of cold pizza. It was tempting to go to Rob's and surround himself in warmth and family.

"Her pesto spaghetti?" Luke asked. He'd loved it for years. Tasted like home, since Rob and Trisha's house had been his home for more years than his own parents' house had felt like anything of the sort.

"Yup. With garlic bread. And chocolate cake for dessert."

Talk about the hard sell. Luke felt guilty. He hadn't been over to visit much in the past month. They'd been so busy, and the way things looked, they were about to get a hell of a lot busier. He needed a break, but as much as he loved Trish and the girls, that wasn't the kind of break he had in mind. It needed to be about release. Nameless, anonymous, quick release.

"Next time, man," Luke said. "I'm in a raunchy mood, and I don't want to be around the kids like this. Uncle Luke's not an asshole."

Rob grinned. "Uncle Luke *is* an asshole sometimes."

"Fuck off." Luke couldn't help smiling back, though. "Give Trish and the girls a kiss for me, okay?"

"Course. Go work off your raunchy mood. Maybe twice."

"Sometimes I wonder if you live vicariously through me." Luke raised his eyebrow at Rob. "You always seem awfully excited when you know I'm about to go find someone to hook up with."

"Yes. I secretly wish I was about to take my job frustration out on some poor British twink's ass," Rob deadpanned.

"I think that might be a little too much, even between you and me." Luke made a face. "I have to say, though, you had me at twink." He gave Rob a casual shove. "See you tomorrow."

"Night, brother from another mother."

"You only wish you had my gene pool."

All Luke got in answer was a shove right back.

LUKE WAS still smiling as he climbed into his car. He didn't know what he would do if Rob wasn't around. Sometimes when it was just them, they reverted back to their college kid banter, and it felt so *good*. He was still a little tempted to sit in Rob's homey living room and let the kids' babble wash over him and Trisha feed him home-cooked food, but he'd been telling the truth. That wasn't what he really needed. Even his aging pizza wasn't going to do it.

It didn't take him long to get back to his flat. The whole damn area had miserable parking, but he managed to find a spot. He locked his car and didn't even bother to go upstairs. He took off on foot for the only place he had any chance of finding what he was looking for.

HE DIDN'T know if it had a name other than random corner gay pub. All Luke knew was there was usually some boy there who had a thing for weathered government types from the States, and he rarely left without getting exactly what he wanted. It was crowded for midweek, way more than usual. He'd have thought the thick, wet cold would've kept the boys at home, but maybe they were all out for someone to help warm their beds, just like he was.

The music was kept at a dull roar, supposedly so people could hear each other speak—as if any of them were actually interested in conversation. It was all about looks, clothes, hair... finding a guy who either did it for them physically or smacked of money. Hopefully both. Luke wasn't rich exactly, but he was a well-paid government employee with a nice suit. He also thought he might have that tall, dark, and handsome thing going. A few of the boys looked his way the minute he walked through the door. Too young, too high, too much trouble. Not interested in any of them, thanks.

"Hi, Damien," Luke said when he got to the bar.

Damien was adorable, but probably not much older than twenty-five. They'd had a brief flirtation a year or so back before Luke decided one or two nights was fine, but he wasn't getting into something real with a kid no matter how good his martinis were.

"Usual?" Damien asked. Luke got his typical sunny grin so he didn't think Damien minded that they'd never gone anywhere past act two of their one-night stand.

"Sure."

"Cold tonight, innit?"

Luke wasn't in the mood for small talk, but he forced a smile. "Good thing it's a short walk from my flat."

"I remember." Luke couldn't tell if it was a jab or not, but Damien kept mixing his drink and then slid it across the bar to him. "On the house."

"Are you serious?" Luke asked.

"Sure. You haven't been in here for a while. If you haven't noticed, you're good for business. Popular with the locals and all that."

"I'm *old*."

"You're *fit*." Damien winked and gestured toward a group of what had to be teenagers checking him out. He still hadn't gotten used to the fact that there were eighteen-year-olds crawling around the clubs in England. Made him feel like a grandpa. Luke took a long swig of his drink and hoped the barely pubescent blondie in the corner wasn't about to make the move Luke thought he might be considering.

"Been busy?" he asked. Better Damien than the barely legal brigade.

"Can't complain." He shrugged. "It's always more crowded in the summer, but I've been busy enough. You?"

"Always." Damien thought Luke worked in a bank. His job wasn't *secret* per se. He just didn't typically tell people he'd met casually. Easier that way. Banker was nice and boring. Nobody tended to ask too many questions about it. While his job wasn't confidential, a lot of the cases he worked on were. Bedside or bar-side, talk couldn't include the suspects he was trailing across England and sometimes Europe. That's why he was Luke Eldridge, banker, if anyone asked.

13

Luke felt someone slide onto the stool next to him. And by felt he meant that in that one second, his whole body *reacted*. Before he even turned around, he knew that was his guy. The one he'd end up taking home that night. Instincts like Luke's took years to hone, and he was rarely wrong.

Their arms brushed together lightly. The hairs rose on the back of Luke's neck, but not like when he sensed danger. It was pleasure. At some stranger's light touch. He tried not to shiver visibly as he glanced over.

"Sorry, man." The guy's voice was honey-soft and cultured. What it wasn't, was English.

Luke turned all the way around to look at the newcomer. "You're American." He grinned.

As much as he was used to the sounds of London, it was still nice to be surprised by a familiar accent on a stranger. A *hot* stranger. The guy was older than a lot of the crowd, probably past thirty, hair the same golden-honey color as his voice, high cheekbones, big brown eyes, long eyelashes, and generous pink lips. Luke wanted to kiss him because, hell, since when had he reacted to someone so quickly and completely? They needed to kiss, if only to test the insane chemistry thrumming through Luke's veins. Probably a little too soon for kissing, though, instincts aside. A few minutes of chitchat oughta do the trick.

"Born and raised. Just moved here a few months ago. You?"

"I've been in London for years. I go back to the States for the holidays sometimes. I miss the sun," Luke answered.

"Where are you from?"

Luke knew the guy didn't care about his origins any more than Luke really cared about much past pillowed lips and his soft, lazy drawl. It was part of the game. Trade a few insignificant details, enough so it was acceptable to take each other's clothes off.

"South Carolina. Outside of Charleston," Luke said.

"New Yorker, myself."

Even if every part of him was appealing, Luke decided he liked the guy's voice the best. He didn't sound like a New Yorker. He talked slow and his voice was warm and a little growly, like he'd spent the night in a smoky jazz bar sipping whiskey. Luke wondered what it would sound like moaning his name. He wanted to know that enough to decide he didn't care about a little white lie. What difference did it make where he was from? All that mattered was where he was going to end up after a few drinks.

"I'm Luke." He stuck out his hand.

"Corbin." Instead of a shake, Corbin picked up Luke's hand and brushed his lips across suddenly sensitive knuckles. More shivers swept through Luke. If his famous intuition was right, and he seriously doubted it was wrong, he and this guy were wasting time they could be spending naked and wound up in each other in his bed rather than a loud pub. But he would do the flirting, buy the drinks. Luke didn't want to make anyone feel cheap unless they were into that sort of thing.

"Can I get you a drink?" he asked. "You look like a whisky sour kind of guy."

Corbin smiled. It transformed his face from pleasant to drop-dead gorgeous. Luke wished he had one of those magical smiles. "You nailed it. What did you say your job was again?"

"I didn't," Luke answered. "Banking. Bit of a bore, but it pays well."

"Security systems and safes. Same." Corbin shrugged delicately. His shoulders weren't broad. He was quite petite actually, but perfectly formed. He would look gorgeous all tiny and golden against bright white sheets. Underneath Luke.

Luke gestured for Damien to come over, and he ordered Corbin his drink. Damien looked a little annoyed, and Luke figured he had a right. It was a tiny bit tacky to rope a new guy right in front of his old one. *Oh well.* Damien probably did very well for himself, and they hadn't slept together in months. There was no way anyone was gonna convince Luke that Damien had just held it in all that time. There was also no way anyone was gonna convince him not to take Corbin home that night either.

Corbin sipped his drink and subtly moved closer to Luke. Luke probably wasn't supposed to notice, but he did. He tended to notice most things. Part of the job, he supposed. He noticed how warm Corbin's skin smelled, and how his sandy hair fell over what really were quite remarkable eyes, warm and gold with long curly lashes that were at least three shades darker than his hair.

"Thank you."

15

"Hmmm?" Luke asked. He'd been caught staring. He supposed it was at least a little bit socially acceptable since they were currently about two inches away from crawling into each other's laps.

"For the drink."

"Oh, you're welcome. I'd like it if you returned the favor sometime." He wasn't going to play coy.

"If you stay around for a few minutes, I will."

"I plan on it." Luke took a sip of his half-empty drink. "You have beautiful eyes," he murmured.

"Charmer," Corbin said with a small grin.

Luke shrugged. "Just noticed. I'm sure most people do."

Corbin rolled his eyes. "You'd be surprised what the men here don't notice. Basically anything outside my pants or my wallet."

"Their loss," Luke said.

He felt weird, like he was being sucked into this thick syrupy vortex. Luke wasn't usually like this, all charm and slick phrases. He didn't have to be. If anything it was typically businesslike. Just a few required phrases, maybe a drink or two before they were on their way. As much as he'd reacted to Corbin, nearly from the first moment, he found himself wanting to take his time and sink into it, enjoy every moment until their clothes were littered on his bedroom floor, and they were a sweaty, sated mess. That moment was coming. He knew it had to be.

Things proceeded for the next half hour. Quickly, but still somehow leisurely. Corbin and Luke scooted closer and closer, ordered each other two more drinks, laughed, leaned, and brushed fingers on wrists and knees until Luke's skin was tingling all over constantly. Luke would've been embarrassed for both of them if he hadn't wanted Corbin so badly by that point it didn't matter what they looked like to a bystander. By the time they left the bar, he was about ready to pull his clothes off right in the middle of the freezing cold, wet, rainy street. Better to keep it together until they got back to his apartment. As far as he was concerned, that moment couldn't come soon enough.

CORBIN WAS breaking all his rules. Well, some of them at least. He never went home with random guys. Well, he *really* never brought them to his place, so that rule was intact, but he didn't tend to go home with guys either, not even when they were the definition of tall, dark, and hot as hell. He'd seen Luke the second he walked in. Like there was some magnet that had drawn his eyes to the bar. Corbin typically reacted to that sort of thing by getting as far away as possible. He'd learned from watching other people make huge fools of themselves and get caught because they wanted something, or someone, way too bad. He couldn't afford to want anything that badly.

If he went by those guidelines, he might be in the middle of making the worst mistake of his life. Somehow, Corbin didn't care.

Luke caught his hand as they walked along and wound their fingers together. It wasn't something Corbin did. Ever. He had a feeling it wasn't something Luke did either. Still, he didn't protest, just allowed his fingers to be twined tight with Luke's and simply existed in the chill, dark night with one lovely point of human contact to ward off the cold. Corbin didn't get all that much human contact, not anything real. He figured he had an hour or so to savor it. Two, if he let it go that far.

"It's that building just up there on the corner," Luke said. He pointed to a building right off Camden Lock. The water was even darker than the night, black and lapping at the manmade banks, lit up with a spattering of reflections.

"Nice," Corbin said. He didn't know much about Camden or a lot of London outside his little corner of it. His time wasn't typically spent sightseeing and getting to know whatever town he happened to land in. Especially not in the freezing cold winter. Luke's place looked nice, though. A bit more exciting than his quiet Notting Hill street.

"I like it. Not very big, but when I want a house, I can go visit my co-worker and his family."

He smiled like he actually *liked* to visit them. Something Corbin wasn't familiar with. The thought of going to see people, of having friends—it was so foreign to someone who spent his life as a shadow, as the bit of mist disappearing around the corner. Shadows didn't have friends. They had families, he supposed, but not the normal type. He couldn't remember the last time his family had Thanksgiving or did more for Christmas than send each other expensive stolen gifts from whatever corner of the world they'd temporarily landed in.

"Here," Luke said and led Corbin into the doorway of his building. His hand was warm on Corbin's back. Even through his heavy coat, he felt it. It was disturbingly nice. For a few minutes, he almost missed the usual call that sang through his blood, the need to touch and weigh forbidden treasure in his hands.

He followed Luke up the stairs. They'd been strangely silent since the pub, almost awkwardly so. It wasn't a bad awkward, more like a first date with two smitten teens. Corbin shook that thought out of his head. Smitten. No. He didn't know why this guy was getting to him so much, but smitten wasn't a word in his vocabulary. If shadows didn't get to have friends, they sure as hell didn't get anything more.

"It's not much, but there's a great view of the water," Luke muttered as he unlocked his apartment door.

Not much. Right. The place was gorgeous. It was quaint and cozy and still somehow modern and beautiful. Luke flipped a few lights on, and Corbin took in the view.

"My mom came over and decorated it for me when I first transferred." Luke made a self-deprecating face. "I guess you never really grow out of being a momma's boy."

"What nationality is your family?" Corbin asked. Out of the dark pub and the even darker night he could tell Luke's heritage was mixed. His skin was pale gold, and his hair was so dark it was nearly black. He had light eyes, though, a mix between gold and green. They were striking with heavy, thick lashes.

"My mom's Lebanese. Dad's a mix of English descent and I think maybe French. A Euro-mutt really."

"So the dark hair comes from Mom?"

Luke nodded. He stripped his coat off and slung it onto a hook on the wall. "Feel free to hang your coat up."

They were being awfully formal. Corbin wanted to get it back, that melting heat from the club that had been pressing the two of them together. He took his coat off and stepped into Luke's body heat. Much better.

"I really wanted to kiss you back there in the pub," he said quietly. He'd known that Luke wanted to kiss him too. There had been something delicious about holding off, delaying gratification.

"Yeah?" Luke's face drifted closer. He tugged a little on Corbin's hair, like he knew how much Corbin liked it. He cupped Corbin's jaw, thumb at his cheekbone. "I think I can probably do that."

And just like that, the heat was back, melting swirling heat as Luke's lips collided with his. Corbin wasn't typically all that into kissing. It was a prelude, something a lot of guys found necessary, something that a blessed few were as eager to skip as him. No, Corbin hadn't ever been into kissing. He thought in one deepening moment, where Luke's mouth melded with his, when his tongue swept in and he nipped just a tiny bit on Corbin's lower lip, that he'd never liked it before because he'd never truly been kissed.

He needed to take control before he lost his mind entirely.

Corbin wound his arms around Luke's neck and tugged him closer. "Where's your room?" He heard his voice go low and husky like he was about to eat Luke alive right there in the living room. If they didn't get to Luke's bed soon, that would be a distinct possibility.

"Hallway. Second door," Luke grunted.

Every time he thought Luke couldn't get any hotter, he was so fucking wrong. Deep growly sex voice did things to Corbin. Things he didn't want to spend too much time thinking about.

They stumbled down the hall to Luke's room, kissing. Corbin wanted more kisses, constant hot, deep kisses. Another thing he didn't want to think about very much. It didn't take them long to undress, fumbling with their own clothes and then each other's like they were eager teens desperate for their first real touches of skin on skin. Corbin hadn't felt such a deep, stinging shot of need in... ever, actually. He had no idea what it was about Luke that had gotten to him so quickly. It was lust, pure and simple, the kind he should walk away from fast. *Not a chance.*

"Bed," Luke muttered against Corbin's lips once they were naked and clinging to each other, trading seeking kisses. "I want you in my bed."

"Yeah. Not going to complain about that one."

Corbin backed across the small bedroom until he felt the edge of Luke's bed hit him in the hamstrings. He clambered back onto it and kept his eyes on Luke, who crawled over him, boxing him in with ropy strong arms and a wide chest. Normally, that would bother Corbin.

Make him antsy and ready to take off. He found himself loving it. He reached up and pulled Luke down on top of him.

"Shit," Luke muttered. "Lemme get shit out before I forget."

Corbin cocked an eyebrow. "Presumptuous," he teased.

"Fuck. Are we not? I didn't mean to—"

"I'm joking." Corbin chuckled and craned his neck up for a kiss. "You gonna fuck me?"

Luke choked. "Jesus, you gotta prepare me if you're gonna say stuff like that."

"Why do you think we're here? Tea?" Corbin chuckled. "We're not that British yet." He couldn't believe he was *joking* with a hookup. Everything about this night, this *guy,* was so off the charts for him. He couldn't be loving it more.

Luke pushed himself off the bed and pulled at a drawer on the nightstand for a moment. Soon he was back.

"Where'd you put them?" Corbin asked. Not that he was impatient or anything. But he'd wanted to feel Luke inside of him since the first time he'd spoken.

"Not yet" was Luke's answer. "I want to take my time with you."

Corbin should've known Luke wasn't the type for a rush job. They went back to kissing, like before, only not like before, because instead of just kisses and seeking arms, it was full-body skin-to-skin contact, and spine tingling touches.

"You're killing me," Corbin said when his lips were puffy and tender and his entire being was dying to see what more pleasure there was to be found in Luke's bed.

"So impatient," Luke chided gently. But he reached to the other side of the bed and produced a small bottle of lube. "I wouldn't want to keep you waiting."

Luke slicked up his fingers and nudged them between Corbin's thighs. "Open," he whispered.

Corbin did exactly that.

LUKE WAS as slow and deep with his fingers as he'd been with his kisses. He dragged out his touches, opening Corbin up with care usually reserved for a nervous virgin. Corbin didn't have the strength to hurry any longer. He only arched his back and lost himself in the sensation of Luke's touch.

"You ready?" Luke finally asked.

"Are you kidding me?" Corbin asked. He dragged a chuckling Luke onto his body. "Now. Or I *swear.*"

"As his majesty commands," Luke said with a smirk. He reached between them, lined himself up, and pushed in with one slick, slow, perfect—*fuck, fuck, fuck*—slide. "Jesus, you feel good," he muttered.

Corbin loved the feeling of a man in him, thick, alive and relentless. It had been one of his favorite things since the first time he tried it. He always craved it, missed it when it had been too long, but still there was something different about Luke. Something more. He wrapped his legs around Luke's hips and tightened them.

"Move. You're gonna drive me crazy," Corbin said. He lifted his head for a deep, wet kiss that ended with a sharp bite on Luke's lip. "Fuck me now."

After that things got a little blurry. It was all sweat and hot skin, slamming hips and breathless praise. He couldn't remember the last time he'd lost himself, felt so good, gave back every drop of heat he got. They felt so good together he swore to God he almost blacked out.

"You're... *Jesus,* I don't want to stop," Luke ground out when he was as deep as he could go.

Corbin felt him there, felt it shiver up his spine and make his hair stand on end. It wasn't normal. He raked his nails down Luke's back and shouted out his release only moments before Luke flopped, sated, on top of him.

"Fuck," Luke whispered.

"No fucking kidding," Corbin said back.

It was nearly five silent, breathy minutes later when Luke finally pulled out with a sweaty kiss pressed to Corbin's lips and muttered, "Be right back."

He returned with a cloth to wipe Corbin down with another kiss, this time cool and on his forehead. It was sweet and considerate, not too typical of his usual one-night stands. Luke collapsed next to him and pulled the covers over both of them.

Corbin froze.

Wait. No. No, no, no, no. No. Corbin didn't do sleepovers, even if the thought of a cozy night and more sex in the morning with Luke made his whole body cheer. No. He started to creep out from under the offending blanket but was stopped by Luke's voice.

"Mmph, where are you going?"

He shouldn't look adorable. Any guy who was as dark and long and gorgeous as Luke shouldn't have the right to look adorable too, but somehow he did. He was bronze and sexy against his pale sheets, but something about the way he reached for Corbin's hand as he tried to slip out of the bed did something to Corbin's insides.

"I figured I'd let you sleep," Corbin said.

"You have to go?" Luke asked. That's when Corbin figured out he wasn't really awake, that somehow in his half-sleep, he already expected Corbin to be there. And that got him more than anything else. He'd never been wanted or needed… or expected. He'd always been alone.

"I guess I don't have to go."

"Good," Luke mumbled. "Stay, then."

He reached out with one of his huge monkey arms and roped Corbin back into bed. Corbin rarely slept naked. There was something too, well, naked about it for him. He needed his armor. He loved his armor. But there was also something about falling into bed with Luke that felt so perfect and easy and right. So he did. Another rule broken. Two. He decided it was fine. Luke, the sexy banker, wasn't going to wait for him to talk in his sleep and give up all his secrets.

Corbin closed his eyes and melted into the big strong arm around him. He was *fine*. Time to sleep.

CHAPTER THREE

April
Malaga, Spain

IT WAS dark, as always. Corbin lived and worked in the dark shifting spaces between dusk and dawn. At least there wasn't freezing wet rain dripping down his collar like there had been in England. The break from constantly being half-soaked was nice. Corbin could already tell London wasn't going to be his home base for the long term.

He crept through the house, empty as he'd meticulously planned it to be, and legged it silently toward the office. *West corner, second floor just past the grand spiral staircase.* Houses like this one always got to Corbin, made him mad in a sense. He could probably afford one just like it, but he'd never seen the need. The excess didn't appeal to him. It was like the people were asking him to come and help himself to some of it. Hell, some of them owned multiple houses like the one he'd silently slid into, filled with jewelry and art and other trappings of gross indulgence. He was more than happy to take the weight off their shoulders—at least the best bits of it.

The alarm had been set, but he'd hijacked the signal for a short window of time with a device he'd paid a ton for in London. The guy he had in the States was better, could've gotten him twice the amount of time with no perceived interruption of signal, but he was still new in town and didn't have the right contacts yet. Beggars couldn't be choosers. As a result, Corbin had six minutes to get in and out before he lost control of the alarm and his motions set it off. Seven, if he was lucky. Corbin never needed luck. He just had to be a little bit faster than usual.

The office where Lord Martindale kept the best of his wife's jewelry and a huge stack of cash happened to be on the second floor.

Another inconvenience, but a small one he'd get around like he always did if something worth working a little harder for was in play. Lady Martindale's heirloom sapphire choker was one of those things. Kept in a wall safe behind a second-rate postmodern oil painting, it was hardly guarded well enough to be a worthwhile challenge. The thing was, Corbin *really* wanted it, challenge or not. He'd been planning to go after it for months. Since the moment he'd touched down in London. It had proved only a small hiccup that she'd taken it with her on holiday.

Again, nothing Corbin couldn't handle. Their safe in Spain was newer, with a digital lock rather than an old-fashioned tumbler. Not much of a deterrent for someone with his experience. He'd been getting into safes just like it since he was a teenager. All it took was a trusty little gadget and a bit of finesse.

Less than thirty seconds later, the safe was open, and he could pick and choose what he wanted. That night, he only wanted the necklace. The rest was nice but not important enough to waste his time.

And there it was. Beautiful.

It shone like a beacon for Corbin's fingers, midnight blue and dripping with diamond accents. It was so clear, it looked liquid. So perfectly cut every stone seemed to sing out his name. He wanted to touch and take, keep it for his own. He'd been lusting after the legendary piece of jewelry for years, ever since he'd seen it up for auction at Christie's. He would've bought it at the time, but why? It was so much more fun to get it his way. Corbin grinned and slipped the necklace into a protective pouch he kept in a zippered pocket of his jacket.

His phone buzzed.

Shit.

He pulled it from his pocket and checked. It was a message from Luke.

They'd seen each other six times since that first night in the pub a few weeks before. Drinks, dinner, more nights in Luke's soft white bed. It was so bad for Corbin. *Luke* was so bad for him. He'd started to become an even bigger addiction than the slinky jewels he'd just had his hands on. Corbin needed to get away. Push Luke to the side until he forgot Corbin existed. After all it had only been a couple of dates and a few phenomenal nights in bed. Not a big deal, right?

Still, he couldn't ignore the pull. He opened his phone and read the message, bag of tools momentarily forgotten on Lord Martindale's rich walnut desk.

Was thinking about dinner tomorrow. Paella?

Spain. Paella. The coincidence got Corbin's heart racing. He nearly dropped his phone. Instead he stared at the screen for long seconds. His hands were all of a sudden shaky, thrumming with nerves and adrenaline he didn't usually have. He got this weird thrill that somehow Luke knew where he was. He knew that was impossible, that it was just a coincidence. Didn't stop his pulse from pounding. Corbin found himself typing an answer.

Can't wait. See you then!

Corbin slid his phone back into his pocket and placed the old pocket watch and the slip of paper with another Covington poem on it right in the middle of the opened safe. There were a few other lovely and quite valuable pieces that clearly Lady Martindale couldn't stand to travel without, but Corbin left them alone. Tempting as it was, it wasn't his style to scavenge like that. Only the best for him. He was about to head out the office door and back to the stairs when the Martindales' alarm system blared to life. He'd taken too long.

Shit. I'm in trouble.

He'd only have minutes before the police arrived. People like the Martindales tended to get quick reaction times. Time to get out of there fast. The window wasn't the safest bet, but it also wasn't visible from the street. He could get out and go around the back to the rental car he'd parked a few streets away. Corbin's contingency plans were usually his weakness. He rarely needed them. There was a first time for everything, he supposed. He was due for a nice massage anyway.

Here goes.

Corbin took a deep breath and shimmied out the window, leaving it open so as not to waste time, and dropped to the first-story garden, landing in soft dirt. *Ouch, fuck.* Soft but not that soft. He dragged himself to his feet and limped out of the dirt. His ankle was twisted for sure. He had to move quickly.

He'd planned to walk right out the kitchen door, just as he'd come in, but there wasn't time to go back and close it. Corbin brushed his footprints out of the dirt and snapped a branch off a bush to drag behind him. Then he crept around the house and down the small hill to the side road. The police would come from the front. He'd made sure of that by calling in a false alarm earlier that week. He also hoped that false alarm would leave them less than thrilled to make another quick trip to the same estate. Couldn't bank on that, though.

Corbin removed his hood and walked casually away from the house. To anyone else, he'd look like he was out enjoying a nice night stroll, but his heart was pounding. That had been close. Far too close. He'd gotten distracted, and distractions were something he couldn't afford. He didn't have the luxury. The necklace clinked in his pocket. He tried to ignore its presence, but he felt it there like a beacon. Like it could be seen from space.

Corbin got to his rental car, purchased under an alias of course, and slid behind the wheel. Safe. Barely.

Luke Eldridge was going to get him locked in prison someday. Corbin wasn't even sure he was sorry.

IT WAS raining. Of course. Luke tried not to let that get to him after all the months and years he'd spent under the gloom. He was flat out exhausted from his day trip to Spain. Useless trip. The scene had looked a little messy, like maybe their thief hadn't had the smoothest of exits, but there wasn't a trace of a print or a tread in the dirt. They wouldn't get that lucky, of course. If they managed to catch this thief, whoever he was, it wouldn't be on a technicality.

He sank down on his couch and put his bag on the floor. Corbin was due any minute, and he was really happy to see him. In a way, he'd rather order takeout and sit on the couch with Corbin to watch a movie, but something about that seemed way too intimate for their, what was it, seventh date? They weren't together yet. Or at all. Luke wasn't that guy who asked that question after a couple of weeks, no matter how great they'd been. He was the one who avoided it.

CORBIN LOOKED gorgeous, as always, when he showed up at Luke's place for dinner. He wasn't an overtly beautiful man, but he was put together perfectly and knew how to dress to show off his small supple frame, how to style his hair to bring out the honey-gold highlights, and what colors turned his eyes into liquid whiskey. Either that, or he was the most effortlessly stylish person in the entire city. Luke would've been envious of Corbin's good looks if he didn't get to touch him. He really liked touching him. His skin was nearly the same melted honey color of his hair and eyes. It made him look like some sort of fey wood creature or something. And when he smiled, he was actually beautiful. And he'd gotten more beautiful with time, not less.

"Hi," Corbin said.

Luke thought he might sound a little bit tired. He totally got it. "Hey there. Ready for dinner?" he asked. Part of him was dying to propose a night in on the couch, but that tended to come before words like "snuggling," and they might fucking do it, but he wasn't going to say it.

"Of course. I'm starved." Corbin looped his fingers through Luke's like they'd been doing since the first night.

Luke wasn't usually one for physical affection. Most of his touches were doled out to Rob's kids, Millie and Daisy, and the occasional hugs when his mother paid one of her rare visits. But something about touching Corbin felt easy. Natural. He didn't want to stop doing it.

"I found a really great Spanish place the other night when I texted you. They have great paella and even better tapas." Luke chuckled. "Ironic, since I was in Spain this morning."

Corbin seemed to tense. "You were?"

That was a weird coincidence. Corbin knew he went all over the place to visit "clients." Spain wasn't any different than Sweden or Germany. "Yeah, the, uh, bank sent me there to do some work with a foreign customer."

"Wow. You've had a long day. We'll keep this dinner short."

"You coming over afterwards?" Luke couldn't help asking. He felt like he hadn't gotten to touch Corbin's skin in weeks, rather than the couple of days it had been. He missed it when it wasn't right there for him to hold and pet. *Fucking moron.* He wondered when a one-off from the pub had turned into someone he missed after a few days. Probably that very first incredible night.

27

It was drizzling at Luke's building, but by the time they'd gotten out of the taxi, it was pouring. He was glad he hadn't decided to take the Underground or his car, which would've meant finding parking or walking from the station. Even the sprint from the cab to the front door of the restaurant was nearly enough to soak their coats through.

"I can't believe this. Is spring always like this here?" Corbin asked when they were panting and shaking their coats off in the restaurant's covered doorway.

"You mean rainy?" Luke chuckled. "This is England. It's almost always rainy."

Corbin made a face. "I guess I should've expected that. Have you been here before or just walked by?" he asked as they went in.

"I came here for lunch the other day with my boss's daughter. We've gotten to be good friends since I moved here."

Corbin elbowed him. "Should I be jealous?"

"The last time I touched a girl was my senior year of high school. I think we're all pretty safe on that front."

Corbin giggled, and Luke found himself smiling. Usually he'd find a laugh like that annoying after a while. Probably not even a whole night. But he loved Corbin's goofy giggle that didn't match his urbane, slick exterior at all. Luke even found himself thinking about it when they weren't together.

They huddled inside the front door, waiting to be seated. The whole room smelled amazing, like exotic sauces and seafood, and wonderful herbs and seasonings. Luke had been looking forward to it all day. More, he was looking forward to later, when they were alone in his bed with the barriers between them stripped to nothing.

"But you just found it?"

Luke nodded "Yeah. Well, Rosie did. It's not really in my usual rounds from the o—bank to home. Rosie assured me it was worth the extra commute."

Luke had stumbled for a moment before catching himself. He'd almost said office. It was getting awkward keeping up the bank pretense. He really liked Corbin, and if they were going to get any more... well, not momentary fling material, it was going to be impossible not to tell him the truth. Luke hadn't ever gotten to that place before. Not even close. He thought he might with Corbin, though.

As unexpected as the whole thing was, he'd just been out for some fun and a bit of stress relief, not finding someone he wanted to *date*. He really thought they could make something of it. And "something" was going to have to include the truth.

The host came with menus to take them to their table. Luke caught her glancing at Corbin more than once. He didn't blame her. The light glinted off his hair and his golden skin, and he looked like he'd been lit from within under the jewel-toned lamps that festooned the ceiling. The effect was gorgeous. Paired with the color of his shirt and the warm ochre walls, he was incredible. He looked like he fit right in this exotic setting.

"What's good here?" Corbin asked when they'd been seated.

"Everything I tried last time. For sure the paella, and I love the olive and hummus tapas. The bread and oil is divine. Everything, really." Luke was apparently hungrier than he'd originally thought.

Corbin grinned. "Why don't we get a few things, and we can share. Sound good?"

"Of course."

They picked through the menu and selected what was probably too many things even to share, but Luke didn't mind. It was cozy and enchanting in the restaurant, glowing against the chilly, wet dark outside. The whole place felt like the inside of a genie's bottle or something, with the rugs and the walls and all the draped fabric. There was a touch of magic. He hadn't had much of that in his fact-filled life. It was really quite wonderful.

They talked until their food came on an array of plates, colorful and spicy. Luke inhaled and smiled.

"Looks amazing," Corbin said. "Thank you for bringing me here."

Luke reached across the table and clasped his hands. "Of course. I'm glad you had some time off tonight."

BY THE time dinner was over, Luke was sleepy and full, and his eyes felt halfway shut. He didn't want to find a cab and take the long ride back to his apartment, but there wasn't any other choice. That was until Corbin brushed the hair off his forehead.

"You look beat, babe."

Babe. That was new. "It's been such a long day." Luke smiled at Corbin. He couldn't help his smile at the endearment he most certainly didn't expect.

"You know, my place is closer than yours is. You want to just come over?"

Luke was surprised. No, actually he was shocked. "Uh, yeah. That would be great. You have an extra toothbrush?" Corbin smiled and nodded. "Then I'll grab the check. Find us a cab?"

CORBIN SIGHED as he left the restaurant to get them a cab. One more rule down the drain, and a first at that. Someone, a guy—*Luke*—was going to be in his place. At least all the art on his walls was legally paid for and the jewelry was hidden in a safe Luke would never find in a million years. Or be able to get into if he did.

Still.

Fuck.

CHAPTER FOUR

Rome
June

"I'M FUCKING exhausted," Rob muttered.

They'd been dragged out of bed hours before dawn to get on the agency's private plane with Kelly and Morgan Laughton, who wasn't very many years out of university and did most of their research for them. Luke hated these kinds of mornings as much as Rob, and there had been plenty of them lately. His ideal version of jetting off to Rome didn't include irritated Roman law enforcement types hovering over his shoulder and missing priceless art. It sure as *hell* didn't include a scrap of poetry on the ground and a tarnished pocket watch hanging from the empty frame, taunting him.

You're not good enough. You won't find me.

Luke was starting to think that. Whoever it was, they had zero leads. Just a string of poem fragments and a growing collection of rusty old watches. He was starting to wonder if they might need to bring in another agency on this one. Waterman was about to sign his release papers if he didn't produce some viable leads. Luke needed something to tell him immediately. Sooner if possible. Their thief was starting to make the whole division look like a bunch of morons.

They were standing in the middle of yet another ornate mansion, different than the first few, of course, but it somehow looked the same as every other ridiculous over-the-top house they'd been in since this new wave of Nightwatchman thefts had started. London, Malaga, Brussels, Amsterdam—beautiful cities that had already blended into a blur of police tape, flashing lightbulbs, and bits of paper with old poetry typed on them. Luke wasn't any closer to the answer than he'd been three months before, standing in that townhouse in Kensington.

Nothing had changed except he was tired of feeling like he never quite got to sleep.

Luke clapped Rob on the shoulder. "I'm beyond exhausted. This has to be the first time these guys have followed protocol, and I wish they hadn't more than anything."

Nine times out of ten, the Italians didn't call his unit in when they stumbled across a case that was flagged. They preferred to keep things in-house even when they weren't supposed to. Of course the one time they did call Interpol involved Luke getting out of a warm bed and onto a plane in the middle of the night. At least Corbin was off in Sweden, Luke thought he'd said, installing a top-of-the-line alarm and safe system. He'd be home later that night, and with any luck, so would Luke. Bed with Corbin was sounding more perfect by the second as he sat there and watched the police glare at them.

"Kelly, did the locals find anything?" he asked. Kelly was better with the local police than he was. He tended to rub them the wrong way. Plus she'd excelled at languages in school, so she often translated for them in other cities. Luke envied her businesslike demeanor that still managed to put the local officials at ease wherever they were. It was a talent Luke didn't think he'd ever have.

"No prints," she read off the form she'd been given. "I'd be bloody shocked if there were. This guy's a pro. Should be if he's who we think he is."

Rob made a face. Luke had known him so long, he got what that face meant. And he agreed. He wasn't who they thought he was. Close, but no.

"There's something about this guy," he mused. "I can't put a finger on it. He's doing everything right. He *should* be the Nightwatchman, but somehow I don't think he is."

"Is it just the age thing? I will admit it'd be hard for a man in his sixties to get in here." She looked out the window, where the climb up an extensive trellis covered in slightly bruised bougainvillea had to have been taxing.

"Agreed. Although if he managed to stay small and in shape, it's not impossible," Rob said.

"No, that's not it. Logically it does make sense. It would be hard for him to keep up his old physical skills unless he was a lot younger than the original caseworkers thought he was. But that's not what I'm feeling."

"What is it, then?"

It was Luke's turn to make a face. "I wish I could *say* what I thought was different. I just have this gut feeling this isn't the same guy we studied back in school. Relative maybe. Protégé. Similar but not the same."

Rob nodded. "If it makes you feel better, I'm thinking the exact same thing."

"So we let the locals finish processing the scene and bag the note and the watch to take back to London?" Kelly asked. She checked her clipboard. Kelly was hardly recognizable without her clipboard and efficient expression. She didn't have as many degrees as him or Rob, but he had no idea what they'd do without her. Probably walk around in circles until they found someone else to tell them what to do.

"That would be great. Then we can get on a plane and go home," Luke said.

He tried not to notice when Rob smirked at him. Like he'd been any better when he first met Trish. Luke nearly choked on that thought.

I just compared Corbin to Rob's wife. I just compared myself to Rob when he met her. Fuck.

Worst part was, he barely wanted to stop the thought from running away even further.

CORBIN WAS still wiping the sleep from his eyes when Luke had called an hour before. He'd had a long night in Rome and a very early flight home, which included the stress of smuggling stolen artwork into England. It was something he was good at, and had many years of practice doing, but somehow it was still nerve-wracking every damn time. He'd gotten back to his apartment and passed out for hours. Until his phone buzzed with Luke saying he was done at work for the day.

His dumb little heart had raced, and he'd suddenly been very awake and unable to keep a grin from stretching across his face. He couldn't help it. Even though Corbin was hiding things from Luke, huge things, Luke still *got* him. They could talk for hours, kiss even longer, and Corbin never got sick of it or him. He'd never had anything in his life that could hold his attention like Luke. He wished he could say it was just the sex, that the way he and Luke were in bed was what kept him coming back for more. It did. But it wasn't just that. Not even close.

AN HOUR after his phone rang with the news of Luke's return, he stood in front of Luke's building and tilted his face up to the watery, late spring sun. It had been a gorgeous morning when he'd stumbled out of Heathrow and into a town car, and it was still gorgeous in the late afternoon. If London was always so perfect and lovely, Corbin would have no problem staying. The wet memory of March and April wasn't far from his skin, though.

"Hey there," Luke said when he bounded out of his building. He leaned over and plunked a kiss right on Corbin's lips. Corbin was still getting used to that, open affection in broad daylight. He supposed Luke was too, if what he'd said was true.

"Hi," Corbin said. He rubbed his hands on Luke's T-shirt. It was soft and silky, almost as nice as the skin beneath it. "What do you want to do tonight?"

"Have you seen Camden Market?"

Corbin shook his head. "I really haven't seen much at all. I'm horrible at getting to know the city I'm living in."

He had this momentary little fantasy of walking around a market with Luke, holding hands, the stuff normal people did. Corbin didn't know where it was coming from, the want that he had to be out in public with Luke where everyone could see them. It was opposite of everything he'd been raised to feel. Still, he wanted it. So far they'd done a few dinners, lots of hours in bed, but the weather and their mutual inexperience hadn't led to very much actual dating activity. As much as he didn't think he would be, Corbin was all for it.

"Then let's do that." Luke reached for Corbin's hand and wound their fingers together. "And there are a ton of places to grab some dinner inside the market if you're okay with that."

"Street food? Adventurous." Corbin raised his eyebrows.

Luke laughed, that sexy, dark chocolate laugh he had that made Corbin want to do reckless things. "It might not be four-star, but a lot of it's really good. You'll survive, I promise. Come this way."

He tugged Corbin toward the bridge that went over Camden Lock, away from Luke's building and into the maze of Camden Market.

IT WAS still beautiful outside by the time they'd wandered through the market and back to Luke's building, ice creams in hand. The evening was getting chilly, though, and Corbin had goose bumps up and down his arms. Cold or not, it wasn't time to go inside yet. Corbin had already wasted a lot of this perfect day sleeping, and he wasn't ready to give up what was left of it. He huddled closer to Luke, who threw his free arm over Corbin's shoulders.

"Freezing?"

"Yeah. I guess it's not quite short-sleeve weather yet."

Luke chuckled. "England newbie. Give it another month and even the nights will be warm."

He squeezed Corbin closer and rubbed his chilled arm. Corbin had to admit it was nice. He'd been admitting a lot of things were nice lately. He tried to imagine his mother's voice, when she found out he was actually *dating* someone. Someone with a regular job. Someone who handled money for a living and probably would not have the most favorable opinion of Corbin's line of work. That little scene in his head took away a bit of the romance of his whirlwind trip into the light of day with Luke, so he pushed it away.

The smells of the market, and the music blaring from the Chinese food stall while the owner belted out Mariah and Britney, brought Corbin back to Luke and how happy he was walking along being a normal guy. It had been hours since he'd thought of his next shiny conquest, which in itself was highly unusual. It was like he'd replaced his first and most familiar drug with another, one that was far more addictive and dangerous. Corbin didn't want to think of the possible consequences. He told himself not to go crazy trying to figure out what could happen in the future. It wouldn't do any good.

"You want to finish these on those benches? Then we can go upstairs?" he asked, gesturing toward his ice cream.

The sun had mostly sunk below the buildings, and the earlier warmth was long gone. He was freezing his nutsack off, but he didn't want to let go of the night. Corbin surprised himself, but he liked being out in public with Luke, not one of the shadows or a spider scuttling around the corner. He liked the fleeting feeling of being a real person. Someone who lived in the sunlight.

"Sure. You going to be too cold?" Luke asked.

"I'll be fine."

"Here. I'm warm. Wear my jacket."

Corbin accepted Luke's jacket with a smile and a nod. Then he bumped shoulders with him and cuddled closer to watch the water and the people, and listen to the off-key pop music from the corner stall. It was really, really good. Better than he thought he could have and nothing he thought he'd ever want. Corbin took a big bite out of his raspberry cheesecake ice cream.

"You're a biter. I don't know if this little thing we have can continue," Luke teased.

"Please. You love it when I bite," Corbin said. He elbowed Luke lightly.

"That was corny."

Corbin rolled his eyes. "And your joke wasn't?"

"Guilty." Luke sat there silently for a few moments. "Okay, this is probably going to be a whole new level of corny, but I'm going to say it anyway."

"What?" Corbin's pulse sped up a bit, happy and trippy and ready to bump its way right out of his neck.

"I've been having a great time getting to know you."

Luke sounded fumbling and sweet. It was such a one-eighty from the dark, rough, suave guy from the first night at the club, the confident well-off man he'd come to know. Corbin liked all the sides of him. The one who was weathered and savvy and used to society, and now this one, who didn't have much experience or skill with dating. He wanted to know more about all of them.

"Me too. I can't believe how fast the weeks have flown by."

"That's kind of what I was thinking. So...." Luke blushed under his golden skin.

Corbin thought he was unbelievably adorable. He couldn't help curling his free hand around Luke's thigh. "What were you thinking?"

"If we made this a little more... official maybe? I don't really do dating. You know that. Not before, anyway. But I seem to be breaking all my rules for you."

Corbin wanted to smile and run and laugh and scream all at the same time. Instead he gave Luke's thigh a squeeze. "Yeah. I've been doing my share of rule-breaking too. What's another one?"

"Is that a yes?"

"I think so. Does that mean you're my...." Corbin wasn't sure he could say the word.

"Boyfriend?" Luke snorted. "Fuck, I feel like a tenth grader."

"Hey, I kinda like that word. Never said it before, at least not about myself, but I think I like it."

"Yeah. Me too. And same. Well, not for years anyway. I tried that back in school, but it was pretty much a disaster."

"That's not very optimistic." Corbin chuckled. He didn't really mean it. He had a good feeling about him and Luke. Sure, it was probably going to end with him disappearing into the night sometime in the near future, but he really fucking liked the way he felt when they were together. He liked the glances they got from people, fond and happy, like they were looking at new love.

"I didn't mean you," Luke said with his soft laugh. "You're not a disaster at all."

"Good. So. *Boyfriend.* Are we going to go in anytime soon?" Corbin's cone had melted while he stared at Luke. It looked a little unappetizing, and he sure as hell wasn't going to finish it after that little talk and the butterflies it had stirred up in his belly. What he wanted to do was go upstairs and kiss Luke for hours. Maybe strip him down and remind him how they'd started. Both of those things sounded a hell of a lot better than some soupy ice cream.

"You don't want that?" Luke looked at Corbin's ice cream and chuckled.

"Shockingly, no."

"Come on, then. Let's toss that and go inside."

37

Luke led him up the stairs Corbin already knew like he lived there himself.

"I'm going to grab a shower. You want to come with me?" Luke asked.

As if he was going to say no to that. "Of course."

They walked through the place, shedding clothes on the floor. He knew Luke would pick them up later when they weren't occupied with getting each other naked anymore. He met Luke in the shower, gorgeous, muscled Luke, who was in the middle of wetting down his dark hair, leaning back into the showerhead that was just a tad too short for him, until his stomach muscles bulged, tense.

"Fuck, you're beautiful," Corbin whispered. "I still can't believe you picked me that night instead of all those little boys who were after you."

Luke opened his cognac eyes, big and gold in the bright light of the bathroom. "Why the hell would I have picked one of them when you were right there in front of me?"

He pulled Corbin to him until they were standing slick skin to slick skin. Luke slipped his fingers lower, between Corbin's cheeks to push gently at his entrance. "Let's get you clean, okay? Then we can work on getting you all dirty again."

Corbin grinned as Luke pulled him the rest of the way under the water.

"That sounds like a perfect night to me."

CORBIN WAS half-asleep when Luke said his name. They'd rinsed off again *after*, and he was cuddled into Luke's fresh, puffy sheets.

"Cor, you still awake?"

Part of Corbin wanted to fall the rest of the way to sleep, but he couldn't resist the nickname Luke had been using for him lately. It made him feel like he belonged, like strolling in the streets or going to dinner. Like he was part of the real world. The world he didn't even know he'd wanted until he'd dipped his toes into it. He doubted he could keep it, but it was nice while it lasted.

"Yeah, babe. I'm still awake. What's up?"

Luke's arm, that had been warm around his middle, slid away, and he felt Luke sit up in bed. "I need to talk to you about something."

Shit. That didn't sound good. Corbin turned and sat up as well. He reached for Luke's hand. "What is it?"

"I don't know how to say this. I never have before." He shrugged.

"You know you can tell me."

Corbin's mind raced. What the hell was it Luke had never told anyone? He didn't seem like the type to keep secrets. He had a family and close friends he talked about constantly. Was he going to tell him... *oh shit*. Corbin wasn't ready for that word yet. Not when he was barely used to the fact that someone had his phone number. He wasn't—

"It's about my job."

Oh. Corbin's heart stood still for one long moment before thumping back to life. That, he could handle. "What about it?"

"I don't work in a bank, Corbin."

Corbin choked. He was glad he wasn't drinking anything; it would've ended all over Luke's perfect white bed.

"What?" Maybe he'd been a little too quick to assume he could handle it. He didn't want to react before there was something to react to, but damn if he didn't want to take off running. As quickly as possible. Not too shocking. Corbin's reaction to most things was to run.

"Okay, that sounded way more dramatic than I meant it to. It's not, like, a *secret*." Luke smiled, but the smile was shaky. A little weird. "My family knows. I, it's not... I'm not CIA, if that's what you're thinking." Luke cracked a smile. "I just usually don't tell people I'm dating. Well I usually don't date at all, and it's really easier not to get into it with guys at the pub, and you know, if I take them home for the night. I don't want questions, but it's not illegal, and I really wanted to tell you since we're not just messing around anymore."

Poor guy looked nervous, sounded nervous too, babbling like that. Not as nervous as Corbin suddenly was. The only kind of semisecret, don't-want-to-talk-about-it jobs people could have were, well, government. There wasn't another choice unless they were talking mafia. Either way it wasn't good. Corbin mentally took about fifty-five dives out Luke's bedroom window. But he had to stay. He had to finish this before he gave into his instincts.

"What do you do, Luke?" he asked. His voice was trembling. Luke probably thought he was angry. He was too freaked the fuck out to get to anger.

"Interpol. I'm an Interpol agent."

"A-and what do you do for Interpol?" He already knew. Spain. Business trips. He *knew*. Part of him had known for weeks, but he hadn't wanted to examine it. Fuck. He had to hear Luke say it out loud.

"I work in an art crimes and jewel theft unit."

Fuck, fuck, double fucking fuck. "O-Oh. Jesus. I don't know what to say to that." *How about can I break the land speed record to get out of here?* He started backing toward the edge of the bed. Only Luke's small, hurt face stopped him.

Corbin had gone from boyfriends and "maybe he's going to say the L-word" to "get me the fuck away from this thing" in less than a minute. He was naked, and he felt even more naked, like all of the people chasing him were staring at him, looking under his skin. In a way it was true. Luke was chasing him. *Luke.* Fuck. The thought that Luke's main job at the moment was probably to catch *him* floored Corbin. He started to giggle. Worst stress reaction ever.

"Why are you laughing? I was sure you'd be angry with me."

"I *am*. A fucking bank, Luke? A bank?" Mad, maybe. Scared as hell? Fuck yes.

Luke shrugged uncomfortably. "It's what I tell all the guys. By the time I knew I wanted more than one night with you, it got awkward. I just…. Fuck, I'm sorry. I didn't know when to tell you. Tonight seemed like the best option after earlier."

"So Rob from the bank? Your best friend?"

"An agent."

"His wife and kids?"

Luke gave him a quizzical look. "What about them?"

Corbin had this overwhelming need to hear all the details. He didn't know why since he was getting the hell out of there at the first opportunity. "That wasn't a story?"

"Of course not. They really exist. Pretty close to here actually."

"And you've told them about me?"

"An embarrassing amount, yeah." Luke must've noticed Corbin shaking. "Listen, what can I do? I really am sorry about this. I've been sorry for weeks. I just didn't know how to bring it up."

"You picked a good time, with my dick hanging out here and shit." Crass, maybe. But he felt so fucking *exposed*.

"Well, so's mine, and you're not the one who just had to admit something."

True enough. The giggles came again. Luke pulled Corbin close until he was practically in his lap, legs straddling Luke's thighs. "Are you okay?"

"Freaked out," Corbin said. It wasn't a lie.

"It's fine. I'm not like James Bond or anything. I told you. I just go after thieves. I'm a good guy."

"You'd make a hot secret agent."

"You don't hate me for lying?" Luke looked really worried. Corbin didn't want to think about the other side of that confession. What Luke's face would look like if he found out who he was in bed with.

"I understand why you did it. I feel really dumb for like, participating in your bank talk. Asking questions about your job."

"Don't. That was my fault. Now you don't have to do it. You know what I am."

"Are you allowed to talk about the cases you're working on?" Corbin asked.

"I'm not really supposed to. Not beyond general detail."

"So tell me. Just what you can. I want to know what I can so I'm not in the dark."

"We catch thieves. Burglars; the kind local police can't handle, international operations. High-profile crimes, high-profile victims."

"Like that lady... I forget her name. The one with the stolen earrings?"

"Yes. Exactly like that." Luke looked down at the bed.

"That's your case?" Corbin tried to look excited but his insides were churning. He had to have confirmation. He had to have proof.

"Yeah. That's my case. Anyway, I really shouldn't say too much about it. We're trying to keep the details under wraps, not that we have many."

"Um. Wow. So, I guess that's all, then?"

41

Luke pulled Corbin tighter. "Yeah. It really isn't that exciting. I just wanted you to know what I was doing when I was gone. I'm not sitting behind some desk transferring money from one millionaire to another. I guess I just... yeah. I wanted you to know the truth. Are we okay?"

"Yes. I'm going to need a little time to wrap my head around it, but I think we're fine."

Until I get the fuck out of here and never come back.

He wasn't leaving right then. Talk about suspicious. He didn't want to do anything to make Luke notice he was acting weird. So he cuddled in Luke's arms and tried to act like nothing was wrong. Odd part was, he found himself drifting off after a few minutes of staring into the dark.

CORBIN WOKE up in the middle of the night with his pulse racing and sweat pouring off him. He'd been dreaming of Luke chasing him down some creepy dark alley, winding around corners, gun waving in the air. He didn't know if Luke even had a gun. Probably. Scary thought. It was his future if he stayed in London. Luke was smart. Maybe not as good as Corbin at the game, but he was smart. Shit.

He crept out from under the covers, and Luke mumbled in his sleep and snuffled into Corbin's pillow. Corbin was sure he'd seen him smile. At least that's what it seemed like. His heart wrenched painfully between his ribs. Fuck. Luke. He had to go. He had to get the hell out of Luke's adorable, charming flat that was sweet and masculine and homey and perfect, and he had to never look back. Not even for a second. Not even standing on the walkway by Camden Lock and staring up into his window pathetically. Especially not that. He needed to get out. Corbin took a step back, away from the bed and Luke and the fleeting happiness he'd reveled in the past few months, and another step toward his jeans. He had to get them on. Get dressed. Get—

"Cor? Where'd you go, babe?"

Babe. Jesus.

The name he'd used on Luke a few times coming right back at him all sleepy and garbled.

"Just thirsty," he lied.

"Oh. Can you bring me a glass of water too?"

Fuck. Luke sounded way more awake. If Corbin reached for his jeans, Luke would notice. Of course, Luke wouldn't have woken up at all if he hadn't spent a pathetically long time staring at him.

"Sure. I'll get you some water."

Corbin traipsed out to Luke's little kitchen and filled two glasses with water while he stared at the counter and berated himself.

He didn't want to leave. That was the real thing. He *wanted* to want to leave. He knew he should leave, but he didn't want to fucking do it. And that was probably the stupidest impulse he'd had in a month full of really stupid impulses. Luke was Interpol. Interpol. Corbin's body and mind, and his goddamn heart while he was at it, didn't seem to care. He was falling for Luke. Actually falling for him. He wasn't sure if that was the giddiness in his belly or the way his chest seemed too big and light and floaty the second Luke was nearby. Whatever it was, he was fucking toast, and he knew it.

He walked slowly back to the bedroom on bare feet with two teetering water glasses in his hand.

"Thanks," Luke said. He reached for the glass and took a long drink. Then he put it down and lifted the covers for Corbin to crawl under again. In that second, Corbin caved completely. Luke's long golden body, smooth and covered with a dusting of black hair—he couldn't leave it. As much as it might get his ass thrown in prison eventually, he couldn't make himself leave.

He crawled under the covers and snuggled his back into Luke's toasty-warm front.

"Damn, you're cold. Do I need to turn up the heater?"

"Nah. It's fine now that I'm under here."

And that was the truth. It was fine. In the dark, in Luke's bed, everything felt perfect. It was just the rest of the time that was a huge-ass mess.

"Thank you for not freaking out on me too much tonight," Luke said. "You handled it way better than I probably would have if I was you."

"I told you, I get it. I wouldn't have known what to do if it was me either."

"You know, I'm really falling for you, Corbin Ford."

And he knew his last name too. Corbin remembered telling him a few weeks back after some wine when it had seemed like no big deal. Good thing his name wasn't in the system. At all.

"I know exactly how you feel," Corbin muttered. That light feeling in his chest warmed, and he threaded his fingers between Luke's, where they were resting on his abdomen.

"I like having you here."

"I like being here," Corbin said. "I always have."

Luke pressed a soft kiss to the back of Corbin's neck. "Can you go back to sleep? I have to get up kind of early tomorrow."

"Yeah. I didn't mean to wake you up in the first place." *No, I meant to take off and run as far as I could and never come back.* Too bad it hadn't quite turned out that way.

"I know. The bed felt weird with you not in it. I think that's what woke me up."

Of course it did. He'd been in it more often than not lately. Corbin simply squeezed Luke's hand. "Night, babe. Again."

"Night, Cor. Sleep tight."

Right. Sleep.

Ironically that's exactly what Corbin did. In the bed of someone who should be his enemy, professionally was the closest thing to a nemesis he had at the moment, was someone who should scare the *hell* out of him, and somehow felt like home. Corbin curled up in Luke's arms and fell asleep like it was the easiest thing to do in the world. When he woke in the morning, it was to the smell of coffee and a note from Luke to make himself at home and grab some breakfast. Even then, in the bright and usually reasonable light of day, he still didn't leave.

Corbin, as he'd said many times to himself in the past few weeks, was utterly and completely screwed.

CHAPTER FIVE

Zurich

LUKE HADN'T been to Zurich before. Never been anywhere in Switzerland. Not that it really mattered, of course. Most of the time when they were in a city, the team flew in and out in a matter of hours, just stopping long enough to do whatever it was they needed to do and maybe sleep for the night if things lasted longer than planned. Typically he was happy to get back to London and sleep in his own bed since the trips were less than entertaining. Luke was constantly telling himself he'd change that.

A few times every winter, he told himself he'd go skiing at one of the resorts in the Swiss Alps, or perhaps to Courchevel in France, but he never made it there. In the summer it was music festivals and hiking and relaxing trips to the beach. Never happened. There was always another case, then another, piling on top of each other in mind-blurring ease until he could barely distinguish one from another.

Except for this case.

They were calling him NW2: Nightwatchman the second. The team had long since decided it couldn't be the original Nightwatchman. That much was certain and was still about all they knew. They thought the thief was a man, or at least a woman who was compact and muscular, and they thought he had either inside knowledge of the first Nightwatchman case or had known the original Nightwatchman. Since they had no clue who the original one was, that was about as helpful as knowing the thief was either an agile smaller man or a muscular woman. Who scaled walls. Someone who could scale walls was probably small and athletic. Luke nearly snorted. That was some Sherlock-level deducing right there. He found himself wishing for the more mundane cases he dealt with in between NW2 strikes. At least

45

there was something there to work with. Something he could *do*. The NW2 case was just an endless series of frustration.

Luke craned his neck to see out the window. Zurich was beautiful as far as he could see—which, as usual, wasn't much. Perched on the banks of a river that led to a lake, it spread out on both sides toward the peaks in the distance. There were green belts up in the hills, and mountains on the horizon. The air smelled fresh and clean. The little bit they'd driven through was charming mixed with modern. He wanted to get out of the hired car and wander down a few of the tight stone alleys, maybe find a cafe to sit at, and enjoy the sun. Maybe, if he had a weekend free soon, he could bring Corbin there for a bit of sightseeing. Best part of being in Europe. Not nearly as far away as everything had been from the States.

Luke couldn't picture Corbin in America. The Corbin Luke knew would've been as out of place there as Luke had first felt in London. Even though Corbin had been in London only for a few months, he seemed to fit, blend into the crowds and become one of the locals. It was an enviable skill not many transplants had. Luke had always felt like the huge American there, even after years of living within the city limits.

"Just another twenty minutes or so," their driver said.

"Thank you," Kelly replied. She leaned back into her seat placidly and fixed a blonde ponytail that hadn't been out of place to start. Luke admired Kelly. She never seemed to get riled up over anything. Not when he and Rob pulled her to some crime scene in the middle of the night at Waterman's request, or when Morgan, their go-to research guy and all around annoying genius, spouted useless facts and figures instead of anything that would really help. He didn't know what they'd do half the time without her steady presence.

"I like it here," Rob said. "First time."

"Me too." Luke and Rob weren't always together on cases. That part of tracking their elusive NW2 thief was nice—getting to work together. But the rest of it was about as infuriating as anything he'd ever experienced. Missing jewels, art, figurines—the already staggering total was adding up quickly. Luke gritted his teeth and prepared for more annoyance.

Rob looked out the window as their town car went over a bridge leading away from the city center. "Might bring Trish and the girls here for a week when we have some time off. Maybe around the holidays. I bet it would be gorgeous."

"I was thinking the same thing about Corbin," Luke said. He'd spent so much time with Corbin wandering around London the past several weekends, a new city would be a wonderful change, not that they noticed much but each other. It was a bit embarrassing, really. Luke's head was still spinning at how fast he'd gone from one-night stand material to the guy who was planning romantic weekends. He didn't really like to think about it. It was easier to concentrate on how happy Corbin made him than dwell on his rapid descent into sap-hood.

"I bet you were," Rob said with a snicker. Kelly smiled behind her hand, and Morgan, who was with them for once instead of on the other end of a phone line, cracked a rare smile. Morgan was great at his job, but he never joined the team for a drink or a meal. He typically kept to himself. Luke figured some work relationships were best kept at that level anyway. If even taciturn Morgan was smirking at him, Luke figured he must look like a lovesick moron. Probably past time to simply embrace it.

THEY PULLED up outside the gate of what promised to be yet another sprawling estate. If nothing else, Luke sure had gotten a tour of some of the most amazing houses in Europe in the past months. Places he'd have had no excuse to see if it weren't for their charming NW2. He thought he might have to send the guy a card.

"We are here," their driver announced. "Herr Gessner and his wife are away on holiday, but their butler can show you where the missing pieces were stored. There are local police on the scene, but they didn't touch anything before they called you."

Luke knew he liked Zurich for a reason.

His team trailed into the house. Quite possibly the best one yet. It didn't have the dark opulence of the place in Rome or the overt excess of Malaga. Everything was understated. Classy.

New money trying to blend in with the society set.

The marbled floors were shiny, the ceilings high and walls covered with eons worth of purchased ancestral art. Everything about the house made him feel like he wasn't meant to be there. The kid from

South Carolina didn't exactly belong. Hell, the butler walking toward them with a stiff back and better posture than most ballet dancers probably had a lot more schooling than he had. More manners too. The butler said something in German, and Kelly nodded.

"He says to follow him, please."

They followed the butler up a grand set of stairs into what looked like a room dedicated entirely to a woman's wardrobe. Luke nearly snorted. And he thought he'd seen everything. Apparently he hadn't even come close. In the room, behind rows of furs and dresses and cabinets and shelves of shoes, was a safe that had been knocked open.

"Don't these people know about bank vaults?" Rob muttered.

Luke gave him a small smile. He went forward to shake hands with the local in charge, and then, without wasting any time, he went for it. There wasn't much to see. Just another scrap of poem and one more antique watch. The locals had dusted for prints, but Luke wished he could've told them not to waste their time. NW2 was better than that. They all knew he was. He did a search of the room and the premises for any clues, but there was nothing. Of course there wasn't. At this rate, they might as well have stayed in London and slept in for once. He wouldn't actually do it, but it was tempting. He gestured for the watch and the poem to be bagged as evidence and shook his head.

"We're not gonna get anything. You want to give it a once over, Morgan? See if there's anything the locals have missed? There usually isn't. This guy is too good."

"Sure. I'll see if I pick anything up."

Luke nodded. "Next time, we're going out to breakfast instead. This is always such a fucking waste of time," he muttered.

"Blintzes?" Poor Rob looked so hopeful.

"Blintzes." Luke punched him on the shoulder. "Next time."

AN HOUR or so later, Morgan had finished his mostly useless survey of the scene and turned up the massive pile of nothing Luke had expected. So his team got back on their plane and took off for London.

"What a waste of a day," Rob grumbled. "The five minutes of sightseeing was nice, I suppose, but other than that, this was shit."

"No kidding. I swear I'm going to tell Waterman not to bother next time. He's not going to leave anything. It's a waste of resources to keep pulling us out to these scenes that aren't going to tell us anything. Just have the locals overnight the evidence to us. I swear."

"Like that would ever happen," Rob said.

"I know." He rubbed his temples with tired fingers. Luke had a headache, creeping in around the edges of his vision. He knew there would be mountains of useless paperwork when he returned about a useless scene in a case that was going fucking nowhere. All he wanted was a beer and some curry and naked Corbin in the shower. With any luck, he'd get all three.

"SO...." ROB gave Luke a quick smirk. Luke knew that smile; it was one he'd gotten very familiar with back in school. It rarely meant anything good.

They were back in the town car on the way to the airport. At least they'd be home in decent time for him to relax and hopefully see Corbin before he passed out.

"What do you want?" Luke asked with a laugh. Rob always wanted something when he smiled like that. A lot of times, it was trouble. At least it had been before Rob settled down and became a husband and a father.

"Actually, it's not me. It's Trish." Luke quirked an eyebrow. "Okay, me too."

"That's what I thought. You always blame Trish when you don't want to take credit for something. What is it?"

"We want to meet Corbin," Rob said quickly. He looked like he thought Luke would get pissed off at him for suggesting it. Maybe fair, since the subject hadn't even come close to being broached. "It's been nearly three months, and well. It's time to bring him to your family."

Morgan and Kelly peered at them curiously.

"Luke's boyfriend. My wife wants to meet the guy," Rob explained.

Kelly grinned. Morgan's expression didn't change much. It rarely did unless he was in the middle of some long-winded explanation that he'd gotten his nerd pants in a bundle over.

Luke's heart clunked a little at that. A lot, actually. He hadn't even thought about bringing Corbin to Rob's house, as much as he sat over there when Corbin was out of town and gushed about the poor guy. And to be fair, he had used the word "boyfriend" last week during dinner. Trish had dropped her serving spoon on the floor. Her mouth had been wide open for a good twenty seconds.

"Trish and I both just want to meet the guy that's turned our Luke into a marshmallow."

"I'm not a marshmallow. Shut your mouth."

Luke grinned at the floor, though. Corbin had done something to him whether he liked to admit it or not. Having someone to come home to sometimes, even if it wasn't all that often with their schedules, made him smile. He wasn't only his job anymore. He actually looked forward to leaving the office a lot of the time. Especially when he was a phone call away from a sweet kiss and dinner with someone other than his best friend's family.

"You bringing him over this weekend? Sunday?" It was their traditional family dinner, but Luke had been skipping it a lot since Corbin came into his life.

"You guys…." Luke shook his head. "Man, I don't know. It's a lot."

"Luke. It's *us*."

Luke shot an embarrassed look at Kelly, who was quite interested in Luke's obvious discomfort.

"It's not just me," he started. "Corbin doesn't really date either. We're both pretty new at this."

"You're going to be fine. You're a grown-ass man, and this is part of what happens when you're with someone. Bring your boyfriend over for family dinner Sunday, and that's final."

Rob had the nerve to look annoyed. *Annoyed.* How dare he? Luke chuckled at that but still, his heart was racing thick and fast and painful in his chest. Corbin was his, only his, and he liked having Corbin to himself, a new part of his life to savor. That's all. But at the same time, Luke had to admit there was something nice about the idea of Corbin surrounded by his little family, his best friends and their kids and the glow of their hectic townhouse. He didn't know if Corbin would like it, or if their messy happy life would be too much for the guy with the pristine flat covered in expensive fabric and even more expensive artwork. Luke figured he didn't have much of a choice after Rob's pointed nonquestion. He had to at least ask.

"I'll call him later," he promised.

Rob gave him the "I've heard that shit before but good try" look and raked a hand through his walnut-colored hair. He'd gotten a few gray streaks at his temples in the past couple of years. Luke, who didn't have any yet, liked to give him shit about it. Trish would usually just swat at Luke and say Rob looked sexy and distinguished.

They pulled onto the private airstrip where their plane was being prepped to take off.

Rob gave Luke a huge smile as they stepped out of the car. "We're not really doing anything right now except waiting until we're cleared for flight. There's no time like the present."

Luke should've known he would say that. Luke would've said it himself. "Fine. I'll call him. Do you have to stand there and hover, though?"

Rob looked like he was trying to decide, then he nodded. "I do. Because I don't trust you."

Luke gave him a mock hurt look. "After all these years? We have *children* together."

"I have children with *Trish,* who you are the loving uncle for. But excellent try. Call him and quit stalling." Rob crossed his arms stubbornly. He wasn't going to move. Luke wished he'd picked a best friend who was more of a pushover.

Luke grumbled but pulled the phone out of his pocket and brought up Corbin's name. He thought about trying to stall some more, maybe fake protesting, but the longer the idea sat in his gut, the longer he liked it. Yes. He'd like having Corbin in the middle of his life in every way, including with Rob and Trish and the girls. He'd like that a lot. He hit call and hoped Corbin wasn't in the middle of something.

"Hey," Corbin said a few rings later. He sounded genuinely happy to hear from Luke. He always did.

"Uh, you busy?" Luke asked.

"Not really. Just reading over an alarm system manual. My jet-set life."

Luke imagined Corbin sitting on the couch at Luke's place with coffee and some technical book on his lap. He knew Corbin wasn't

51

there, but the idea was way nicer than he wanted to admit. "Sounds riveting."

Corbin laughed softly. "You have no idea. I'm glued to the pages."

Luke found himself grinning. Kelly gave him a speculative look. He figured that wasn't exactly common on the job scene. "What are you doing this weekend, like, Sunday night?" he asked.

"I was hoping something with you," Corbin said. "As long as you don't have an, uh, well... am I allowed to talk about it?"

Luke chuckled. "Sure, to a point. I'm hoping I don't have to deal with any casework at all this weekend. If not, are you free for dinner?"

"Yes. Of course."

Luke heard the smile in Corbin's voice. Made him want to smile too, if that wouldn't turn into him looking like a dumb-ass in front of Rob. Any more than he already did, at least. "Um, would you be free for dinner at a friend's house?"

"Friend?"

"Rob. And his wife and kids. They want to meet you."

Corbin was silent for a little while. "Really?" he finally said.

"Yeah. Actually, quite a bit. Rob's been harassing me about it."

"I've never done the 'meet the friends' bit."

He sounded a little nervous. Hopefully good nervous and not "you're never gonna hear from me again" nervous.

"Actually it's more like meet the family. He's the closest thing to a brother I'll ever have. My mom even calls him on his birthday."

Corbin coughed. "That made everything much less intimidating, if that's what you were going for," he drawled.

"They'll love you. I mean, you can say no if you really want to, but I swear they'll love you."

"Then how can I resist?" Corbin said. "Of course I will. What can I bring?"

"Oh, Trish always cooks. I usually bring wine and treats for the girls."

"I can do wine. So... this weekend. Dinner with your family."

"Yeah. What are you doing tomorrow?"

"Man, I wish I could say I was coming over, but I have a quick job in Paris. I'll be back around ten. You mind having company to watch the news?"

Luke couldn't help what was probably a goofy melting expression even though Rob was in the background mocking him for all he was worth. Bastard. "Yeah. I'd love it. I'll see you then?"

"Sounds perfect."

"'Kay, I'd better go before nobody on my team respects me anymore." Luke grinned. A nervous giggle rose from his belly, but he swallowed it before he had to clap a hand over his damn mouth. Rob smiled fondly and shook his head.

Corbin chuckled. "See you tomorrow."

IT HAD been raining all morning. Of course it had. But Luke barely noticed. The rain was a part of him by then, after all the years slogging through it to crime scenes, trying to find places to park, wiping it off of his face and his coat. So yes. It was raining. He also didn't care. All Luke could think about was that Corbin was waiting for him at his place. They'd spent all of Saturday together, but Corbin had gone home earlier to get some work things settled. It had been an embarrassingly long four hours.

Luke had decided to pick him up again so they wouldn't have to split cab fare, and also because, well, he was taking Corbin to meet Rob and Trish, and that was important. It was a first, obviously. He wanted to treat it like the big step it was.

Only a short jog and Luke was at his car, which was a good thing. Traffic was heavy for a Sunday, which was probably due to the rain. Luke was sitting in the unexpected traffic. It would take him three times as long to get all the way to Notting Hill and back as it would've to go straight to Rob's, but he didn't mind.

Luke had been stopped at a light for a few seconds when he noticed the big ad for Rolexes plastered to the side of a building. He was starting to hate the sight of watches, even normal ones. Luke gripped his steering wheel tighter and tried to push NW2 out of his head. Zurich had been such a fucking waste. They had nothing other than another untraceable old watch, another piece of paper with some meaningless poetry, and a big pile of jack shit.

Luke was beyond annoyed. He wondered if there was any point trying to trace him. It seemed like an impossible chase. Their new thief wasn't the Nightwatchman—Luke's gut was certain of that even if the evidence didn't point to anyone else—but he was damn good. They weren't going to catch him unless he slipped up.

LUKE WOUND his way through wet streets until he was in front of Corbin's building. It wasn't all that far, distance wise, but the traffic had been a bitch. Consequently, he was nearly fifteen minutes late. Corbin popped out of the door as soon as Luke pulled over and jogged through the downpour to the passenger side.

"You really didn't have to pick me up. I know how to use the Tube, you know," he said as soon as he got in.

Luke hugged Corbin and pressed a kiss to his lips. "I know. I want to."

"We being all formal tonight?" Corbin asked with a smirk.

"I guess. This is new for me, you know. Don't give me shit." Luke was *not* going to make a pouty face, fucking hell. No. He let Corbin wind a few fingers around his and squeeze.

"Oh, it's more than new for me. It's an absolute first. I don't do families. I'm sure you've figured that out."

Luke didn't do anything more than one-night stands. At least not until Corbin had showed up, so yeah, he'd figured as much. "Me neither. You're not going to bring your parents out here or something. Are you hiding them in that posh apartment of yours?"

Corbin choked out a laugh. "No. The Atlantic is barely enough space between us, thanks. Any less than that, and I'd be going insane."

"Ouch." Luke grinned. "Good thing, though. Rob and Trish I can handle. Your parents would terrify me. Still. Harsh."

"I don't mean anything by it." Corbin laughed. "I love my family, but I love them at a distance. I don't really want to go back to the States anytime soon."

"I'm glad," Luke said. And *he* really fucking meant something by that.

All these pictures had been flashing through his head ever since he and Corbin had become more than two guys who'd had really good sex a few times. It kinda fucked with his head. He'd never seen himself settled, on the couch watching movies or walking through the market holding hands, going to dinner with Rob and Trish, but he was that guy now, in record time, and it was really fucking weird. The weirdest part was how he'd sunk into it like nothing was out of the ordinary, like it was so easy to be with Corbin he didn't have to have a mental freak-out every ten minutes. He had to say he liked it.

"HEY, YOU want to go grab a drink after dinner?" Corbin asked. "I have a feeling we're both going to need it after the interview section of the evening. At least I will."

Luke pulled Corbin's hand up and bit at his knuckles. Then he kissed them. "Rob and Trish are going to be totally cool with you. I swear. There isn't going to be an interview."

"Right." Corbin's face said he believed that about as much as... not at all. "I've seen movies. There's always an interview."

"They're gonna love you." Luke resisted the urge to ruffle Corbin's hair.

"When was the last time you brought a guy to meet them?"

"You know I never have."

Corbin made a face. "Exactly. You have no idea how they're going to act."

"They wanted to meet you, so I'm sure it'll be friendly."

"They wanted to see if I was good enough for you. And because I want them to like me, I said yes. I'm a little freaked out about the whole thing, but I'm still going to do it."

"You're gonna do great." Luke squeezed Corbin's hand and left it on his lap. It was a little awkward at first. He didn't have a lot of practice holding someone's hand while he drove. But he liked it too much to let go.

"Where do they live?"

"Still in Camden but about a half mile from me. It's a nice area. A little less busy and a park only a few blocks away for the girls to play in. I really like it."

"Why don't you get yourself a townhouse there?"

Luke shrugged. "I guess it always just seemed too family-oriented. I couldn't see myself in a family style townhouse in that area all by myself and, well, I wasn't going to have their life for sure."

"But you can have that life, you know. If you want it. Not that your place isn't gorgeous, because it is."

"I like it a lot better lately." Luke felt himself blush. "Fuck, that was cheesy. Please strike it from your memory immediately."

Corbin smiled hugely. Luke pretended he didn't see that. "I'm not going to. I like being there. It feels more like a home than my place."

"Less expensive for sure."

Corbin poked his thigh. "Like that really matters. You know it doesn't."

"We're here," Luke said and gestured to one of the stone townhouses a few buildings away. It didn't look much different than any of the others. That was something he'd had to get used to when he first moved to London from the States. But it was inside where the personality was. Trish had decorated the walls in vibrant colors and added plush furniture, brought some of home to the old column of stone.

"I like it," Corbin said.

Luke chuckled. "How can you tell? They all look the same."

"I don't know. Just a feeling."

CORBIN WAS terrified. He'd been trying to hold it back the whole time he was in the car, but he wanted to do nothing more than bolt the hell down the street to whatever Underground station was closest and get lost in the weekend crowd. It wasn't meeting the friends and family, although that in itself was terrifying. It was Rob. And Luke. Interpol agents. Men who should've had his number weeks ago. He felt like every breath he took in Luke's presence might be the one to give him away. Every moment they got closer and more intimate might be his last.

The worst part was, his will to escape waned daily, even when he had random moments where he wanted to take off. All he had to do was think of Luke and, well, he didn't want that anymore. It was insane. He knew it. Absofuckinglutely insane. One snap of Luke's fingers, and he could spend the rest of his life behind bars, just for what he'd stolen since they met. If they got into his safe at the apartment, well, another lifetime at least. Maybe two. He'd lost his mind. There was no other explanation. Still, he stood in front of Rob's house ready to meet the friends, play nice, and get even closer to the guy who would probably pull his noose without a second thought if he figured out who Corbin was.

He followed Luke through the gate and up the stairs to Rob the Interpol agent's townhouse, where he might easily meet his doom. Luke didn't bother to knock, just threw the door open and announced his presence. He gestured for Corbin to follow him inside. Corbin's heart was jammed right up in his throat, but he followed.

Rob's coat was hanging on a hook, his badge right there, sticking partially out of the breast pocket. There wasn't a gun—that was hopefully locked up away from the kids—but if Corbin wanted any sort of physical reminder of who Luke and Rob were, and how stupid he was for being there, well he had it. *Insane. You're insane.* In an instant they were bombarded by five and a half feet of voluptuous brunette. Luke laughed and fielded an enthusiastic hug. Corbin was surprised when he got one himself.

Trish pulled him and Luke the rest of the way into the house. It was really nice inside, with multicolored walls, a huge fireplace in the living room, and bright hardwood floors. There were kids playing in the background. As soon as they heard the door shut, two little girls were squealing toward them, shouting for "Uncle Luke" at the top of their lungs. There were hugs for Luke and shy waves for Corbin. Trish gave Corbin another hug and tugged him close. She was pretty and round, with wild curly hair that was tawny with streaks of gold. Her jeans were a little tight, and her shirt was stained with whatever the girls had gotten into earlier. Corbin thought she was beautiful. He thought everything about the place was beautiful. Except for the badge in Rob's pocket and everything it stood for.

"I'm so glad Luke met you," Trish whispered into his ear as she let him go.

Corbin was taken aback. He was new, and they didn't know him. How could she be glad he was in her friend's life so soon? It didn't seem like anyone would be that welcoming. Or should. Rob wasn't. He shook Corbin's hand and welcomed him, but there weren't any hugs or big smiles, no whispered encouragement from that one. Probably because of what he did for a living, or maybe he was just the protective type. Corbin totally got it and wasn't even surprised, but he knew where his work lay if he wanted to make Luke's best friends his own as well. And he did.

That was the scariest part. Not Rob's job, or Luke's, but the fact that Corbin wanted into their life. He didn't see a way for that to happen once they found out who he really was. *What* he really was. And there was no way they couldn't find out. It just... wouldn't work. He got a cold, slippery drip of fear down his back at the thought of it. He really wasn't going to get to keep this. Any of it. There was just about zero chance. None. Corbin shook out the fear and decided he'd enjoy it while it lasted. Until he had to leave, whenever that might be.

IT WAS dark by the time they left Rob and Trish's house, full and smiling. Corbin couldn't believe how charmed he was by people he'd been determined to be terrified of, people he'd expected to keep at arm's length. Or further. A nice football field would do. But they'd been sweet to him after the initial grilling and Rob's early reticence, and the whole night had that encompassing light feeling he'd come to associate with his time with Luke. Addictive. Just like the rest of it.

Luke wrapped an arm around Corbin's shoulders. "I told you they'd love you. You even got Millie to fall for you, and that little one's a tough cookie."

"Yeah?" Corbin's grin spread.

"Yup. She doesn't like anyone at first usually. Where to?"

"Are you still up for that drink? I'm a little too wired to go chill at home just yet." Corbin's blood pressure had cooled down a lot after he realized Rob and Trish were going to accept him, but there was still a lot of adrenaline pumping through him from being "on" for so many hours. It would be nice to get some of the jitters out before they went home.

Luke's lips quirked in a small smile, and he nodded. It took Corbin a few moments to realize why. He'd called it home. He had called Luke's place home. And then he'd thought of it as home. Without a single moment of hesitation. Jesus. It seemed to make Luke happy even though Corbin was about ten seconds away from panicking.

"You okay with the corner pub?" he asked.

"Sure."

Oddly, they hadn't been in there since the night they met. Maybe it wasn't a place either of them had needed after that. But it would be fun to go out in public and have a drink or two. Corbin wouldn't mind rubbing Luke in all the little twinks' faces, either. Yeah, he had the guy they'd all been salivating over. Too damn bad for them. Corbin had watched them watching Luke that first night, but Luke had been oblivious. Either that or he really wasn't into any of them because he'd spent a gratifying amount of time staring at Corbin's eyes. Yes, it would be fun to go back there.

They parked Luke's car in its customary place, then walked down the street to the pub. The bartender greeted them with an insincere smile and a long look at Corbin, who was clearly the same guy Luke had left with nearly two months before. Yep, he could suck it too. Corbin put his hand low on Luke's belly, fingers grazing familiarly right over his belt. *Mine.* That moment of possessiveness shocked him. He'd never felt like that before, either. Shouldn't have surprised him it was over Luke.

"You okay with your whiskey sour, babe?" Luke asked.

"Yeah. I'll grab us a table. Is that cool?" Corbin asked.

"Course." Luke brushed a kiss over his lips and turned to the bar, where bartender boy was downright pissed-looking. He managed to wipe the bitchy look off his face and give Luke a professional smile. Still glared at Corbin when Luke was rifling around in his wallet for cash.

"That was awkward," Luke said when he got to the table with their drinks.

"How come?"

"Used to have a bit of a thing with him. It was a long time ago, though. I guess he hasn't quite gotten over it. I feel a little bad."

"What did he say to you?"

Luke's cheeks went pink. "Nothing. He was just being snarky about you. Really not worth repeating."

Corbin took a long appreciative sip of his drink. "It's okay. Doesn't mean anything, does it?" *Suck it, bartender.* Corbin had never pretended to be mature. At least he managed not to look over at the guy and smirk.

Luke put his hands over Corbin's and shook his head. "Course not. I'm here with you."

"So, you're sure Rob and Trish liked me?"

For that he got another indulgent smile. "Yes, I'm sure. I've known Rob since we were kids. I know when he's faking it, and he wasn't at all."

"I'm really glad. I was worried."

Luke leaned forward. "You know what? I wasn't worried. And even more, I loved watching you with them. It was like the longest four hours of foreplay in my life."

Corbin reached over and swatted at Luke. "I was with your friends. And *children*." He laughed.

"I know! But it was so hot watching you slip into my life like that. You fit in like you've been there all along. You have no idea what that did to me. I swear."

"I think I can probably guess." Corbin gave Luke his best sly smile.

"And *I* think we're probably going to leave here after one drink."

Corbin fake gasped. "Do I look like I'm easy?" he joked.

"Yeah, I think so. But not as easy as me."

They were such dorks. He didn't even give a shit.

"You know, that first night." Corbin chuckled. "I can't believe how many drinks it took you to ask me to go home with you."

"I didn't want you to feel cheap," Luke said. "You didn't seem like the kind of guy I should treat like a quick fuck. I kinda liked drawing it out." Luke scratched lightly at Corbin's forearm.

Fuck. Talk about foreplay. "I was ready to go with you after the first sip."

"Didn't even take that long for me. I felt you next to me, hadn't even looked yet, and I knew you were the one I wanted the rest of the night."

Corbin played with Luke's fingers. "Probably didn't expect to have me here months later."

"No. But I'm happy to be proven wrong."

"C'mon. Let's finish these drinks and go. I think I'm going to be a cheap date tonight."

"Yeah?" Luke had that smile on his face, the one Corbin remembered from what seemed like years ago, another lifetime. It was dark and sexy and totally not like the dorky guy he'd gotten to know and I—

I didn't just think that word. No.

He had. A swooping, shaky lightness hit his belly hard. Corbin tried to smile through it. "Yeah." Corbin shot the rest of his drink down hard and fast. "Let's go."

Don't think love, don't think it. Too late. Corbin, Jesus. You're screwed. He was falling in love. He was in love.

He hadn't ever come close to thinking he *liked* someone for more than a fleeting moment, and there he was totally head over heels. He didn't want to think about how it was the worst possible choice. He didn't even care. He just wanted to get Luke home and into his bed.

Luke shot his drink down too and stood, reaching for Corbin. "C'mon. Let's go. I think I have something back at my place I need to show you."

Corbin giggled at that. "That was *horrible*."

"You loved it."

I love you.

Corbin didn't answer, just grabbed Luke's hand and let him lead the way out of the unassuming pub that might have changed both of their lives irrevocably. He was vibrating, he wanted kisses, he wanted Luke. The need hadn't diminished at all. Rather, it had grown every single day.

ON THE walk back to Luke's place, the ground seemed to float somewhere a few inches under Corbin's feet. He didn't know if it was his realization flowing through him all scary and hot and wonderful or just the anticipation of what was to come.

They slipped through Luke's door already taking off shoes and dropping keys. Corbin couldn't wait to get Luke into bed.

"I never get sick of this," Corbin murmured, almost to himself. He smiled into Luke's neck and nibbled at the muscle that went up the side.

"Me neither. Need your skin."

Corbin mumbled agreement and stripped his shirt off, his jeans, his briefs, until he was naked and crawling across the bed he'd started to think of as his. "C'mon. Hurry," he said to Luke.

Luke pulled his shirt off too, barely taking his eyes from Corbin the whole time. He fumbled with his zipper and tripped onto the bed, pulling at his final sock. Corbin laughed and hauled Luke into his arms. It wasn't easy to laugh and kiss at the same time, but it might have been the best feeling in the world. He wrapped his legs around Luke's bare, muscular hips.

"I want you," Corbin muttered.

"Like last time? When I brought you home from the pub, and we were so desperate for each other we couldn't stand to wait?"

"Sounds about like every time." Corbin was constantly lusting for Luke's body, for his touch, for his kiss and taste. He loved having a big warm man all to himself.

"I don't think I'm going to let you be impatient tonight," Luke said. He pulled away and shimmied down, kissing along Corbin's chest, stopping to suck on his nipple. "You're going to have to wait."

"I don't do waiting that well," Corbin breathed. "I'm sure you've noticed."

"Too bad." Luke lifted his head and grinned, then went back to his slow journey over Corbin's skin. He licked and tasted, kissing everywhere that felt good, but nowhere that Corbin needed.

"Why are you *teasing* me?" Corbin whined. "I want you." He reached down and tried to pull Luke up, so he could wrap them together and feel Luke's weight pushing him down.

Luke scooted even farther down and ran his hand up the inside of Corbin's thigh. "You want my fingers?"

"I don't fucking care. Anything." He didn't know why he was so on edge. Why he needed it so damn bad, but he did. He wanted to be filled. He needed that connection.

"Why do I always listen to you?" Luke asked.

"Cause you want it too. Come up here." Corbin grabbed at Luke until he hovered over Corbin for a long, slow kiss. The he reached into his drawers for a condom and the lube they'd need to replace soon.

"I wanted to take it slow," Luke said. "Show you how much tonight meant to me."

"I know. Tomorrow, okay? I just need you."

Luke looked like he was holding back a shy grin. "'Kay."

He slicked his fingers up with lube and gave Corbin the minimal amount of prep before Corbin was pushing at his hand and making impatient noises in the back of his throat. It wasn't enough. The connection wasn't deep enough that way. He needed *Luke*.

"Now, now. I'm ready," he said.

Luke made quick work of rolling on a condom and applying lube. Then he took Corbin's leg and slung it over his shoulder. "I love how bendy you are," he said. "So fucking hot." Then he lined himself up and sank in slowly until he was thick and deep inside Corbin.

Yes. That's what I need.

Corbin rolled his hips. "You feel perfect. Fuck me, babe. Now."

Luke didn't hesitate. He angled Corbin exactly right and rolled his hips deep. Corbin felt each stroke all the way up his spine in tingles and sparks that tightened and swirled in his belly. "Every damn time," Luke ground out. "You feel like fucking heaven."

Corbin couldn't answer. He grappled at Luke's back and moaned and tried to pull him closer. As close as they could get. He loved that Luke knew his body, knew exactly what to do to get him hot. What would work every damn time to get him to come. Luke pulled out all his best tricks. He hit Corbin's prostate at exactly the right angle, every stroke. He kissed him, breathless and full of awe, and whispered encouragement into his ear.

Corbin's orgasm hit him hard and quick. It took him by surprise. He reached back and grabbed Luke's headboard, arched his back, and shouted as the contractions echoed through his belly. He squeezed his eyes closed and bright spots danced behind his lids in the dark. For a moment, he held his breath, time suspended, until he heard Luke shout out as well, shudder, and collapse onto him.

THEY LAY there limp and sated until Luke pulled out and rolled over for a moment to wrap up the condom and throw it away. Then he was back, pulling Corbin up against his chest.

"Mmm, that was amazing." Corbin barely had any breath to speak, but he wanted to say something. It deserved *something*.

"It was." Luke pressed a sweaty kiss to the back of Corbin's neck. "Sleep?"

"No shower first? I'm a little gross." Corbin felt he should protest, but he really didn't want to move.

"Morning. Sleep." Luke pulled Corbin in tight and draped his thigh over Corbin's legs in case he got the idea to move. Corbin was quite fine with the arrangement, after all.

"Night, babe."

"Mmph. Night."

HE FELT like he'd been asleep for five seconds when Luke's phone squealed loud and angry in the dark silence of the bedroom.

"Luke, babe. Your phone's going off." Corbin shook Luke, trying to get him to wake up. He didn't want to wake Luke. Every time Luke's phone rang, Corbin's heart leapt into his throat and tried to escape.

"Mmph. Mute it."

Corbin was so damn tempted to listen to him, but it was work. He saw the name lighting up Luke's screen like a warning siren. They'd keep calling until they got Luke if it was important enough to call at... Jesus. Four in the morning. "Babe, it's Morgan. He probably needs something."

Luke grumbled and slapped around his nightstand until he landed on the phone. "This better fucking be good. It's the middle of the goddamn night." His voice even scared Corbin. Corbin rubbed Luke's back that had gone from sleepy and soft to tense in seconds. He heard Morgan muttering but couldn't make out the words.

"What are you saying?" Luke finally asked.

"I'm saying I think you'd better get down here and look at this," Morgan said clearly through the phone. Corbin thought his heart might stop. *Fuck, fuck fuck.* "We've finally got something on NW2."

CHAPTER SIX

LUKE DIDN'T want to be awake. He didn't want to be anything but in bed with Corbin reliving the night before. The very *long* night that had ended only a couple hours ago. The part with Rob and Trish had gone perfectly. They'd loved Corbin. Everyone had laughed and eaten and had a great time. Of course there was also the bar, after the bar, cuddling under the covers after that. The whole thing was, well, it was over, effective the second his damn phone had rung.

The phone call from Morgan was harsh after the haze of how perfect things had been. A kind of jerk back into the reality Luke didn't feel like dealing with. Ironic that Luke's job used to be his life, and now it seemed like it was what got in the way of his life. He didn't know if it was better before or if he'd been fooling himself that he was happy.

By the time Luke got to the office, nobody else was there yet. Obviously. Because they weren't insane. Luke didn't know why Morgan had been there in the first place to even call him in. Who would be up at four in the morning on a Monday? Luke placed his extra-large coffee on his desk and sat on the chair for a moment before he hauled himself back up and toward Morgan's office. He tried to get excited about whatever it was Morgan thought he had, but he was too damn tired and had given up the idea of finding NW2 weeks before.

Luke found Morgan hunched over his desk, computers on. His hair hadn't been brushed or washed, and Luke was honestly not sure he had changed clothes since Saturday when Luke had spent a few lame hours at the office filling out reports and waiting for Corbin to get back to London. Morgan looked like he hadn't slept at all since then.

"Morgan?" Luke finally asked when he realized Morgan wasn't going to notice he was standing there. The way the poor guy looked, he probably wouldn't notice a tsunami coming right for him. Morgan jumped, then jittered his way out of the chair. He ran a hand through his greasy hair until it stood on end and twitched like he'd had about a hundred too many coffees.

"You okay, man?" Luke asked. He and Morgan hadn't ever been close, but he wasn't about to let the guy have some sort of stroke on his watch. He figured he'd get whatever info couldn't wait until seven and then send him on his way.

"Yeah. Good. I'm fine. Good. Yeah." Morgan shook his head. "I found something. Can't *fucking* believe I missed it. But yeah. Here. Look."

For a guy who was usually methodical and a little bit cold, Morgan's tone was jarring. So was the swearing, which was completely out of character. He sounded half-drunk and more than a little strung out. Luke decided it was probably too much caffeine and a lack of sleep. If it was anything else, he didn't want to know.

"What is it?" Luke asked.

Morgan started laying the sheets of paper in his hand across his desk. Luke looked at them. Turned out they were the printed poems NW2 had left at each scene, blown up to the size of printer paper.

"Morgan, we've looked at those already. Many times."

"Look again." Morgan stepped back and let Luke have the table.

Luke scanned the sheets for watermarks, initials, anything. There wasn't anything there, just like there hadn't been the first time around. They were just poems. He knew the team had done the work. They'd been tested for prints, the origin of the paper, and nothing had been identifiable.

"What am I looking at here? I see the same thing I've seen every time."

Morgan slammed a finger down on one of the sheets and then pulled a book of poems out from underneath the pile and turned to a marked page. "This. *Shit*. I can't believe we didn't catch it weeks ago."

Luke looked at where Morgan's finger was jammed against the paper. It was the poem from Nice in France, he thought. The scene before last. Then he looked at the book. Same words. Same poem. "What? I don't see anything."

"Look," Morgan repeated. Luke noticed faint lines under a few of the letters, like they'd been copied over a few times—by Morgan he assumed, since none of the original poems had had any letters marked at all. In fact, the first letter of the second word of every line was underlined. As he read them out loud, they spelled—oh holy fuck. They spelled *Zurich*. Wait… no. He looked again. Yep. Zurich. And that was weeks before they'd gotten the call that NW2 had hit the exact same city.

The poems weren't just calling cards. They were warnings.

"He's leaving us clues, Luke. NW2 is *telling* us what city he's going to hit next." Morgan's finger trembled on the paper, crinkling it slightly.

Luke felt like he was going to puke. "You sure that's not a coincidence?" Luke asked. "Like with that poem?" The likelihood of that happening was slim to none.

Morgan shook his head. "No, not a chance. And look. Here's the one we found *in* Zurich."

Touch languid on silk-brushed skies
Morning orange and flame we seek
Then north fires rage and die and fall
With desperate pyres
Tired of charred sad hope
That never will fall so soon

The letters were underlined again, first letter of the second word of each line. L, O, N, D, O, N.

Oh, shit.

If the poem was right, NW2 was about to hit London again.

"Are you sure?" Luke said. "Are you absolutely sure?" His mind was blown. How the hell could they have not noticed?

"I'm very sure, and I'm kicking myself over here. Back when we found the first one"—he moved a paper—"See, here? I thought he'd just split the middle lines to fit on the square of paper, but look. It says Malaga." Luke studied the original poem, the one they'd found in Kensington all those months ago, and clear as day, the first letter of the second word in each line spelled Malaga, the next place NW2 had hit.

WIND MOVES harsh on Autumn wings
Blue as heart and flowers to stone

Rend love from love
and ash from earth
'Til God's seed is shriveled and spent
Empty and wasted with regret

Morgan looked angry. "I thought it was just for convenience on the first one. I can't *fucking* believe it. And then the rest of them I didn't even look all that closely at if there were lines cut in different places, since he'd split a line with the first one. Figured they were just calling cards and nothing more, like with the original Nightwatchman, that he was being careless with where he put his words. I didn't even run them through any programs because I didn't think there was any code to find. But they're all clues. Obvious clues at that. Every single one of them."

Morgan tapped each sheet as he read off the names. "Malaga, Rome, Berlin, Oslo, Nice, Zurich—he's been leading us to the next location all along. He must've just... I don't know. Decided on the right stanzas to scramble. Ones he didn't have to make big changes to. I'm sorry it took me this long to figure it out."

Luke was surprised it had. None of them had noticed, and now that he knew, it was so *obvious*. Maybe they'd all gotten so used to having nothing to work with, they'd been careless with the details. Not even a detail. A huge beacon. *Fuck*. Luke started flipping through the book to all the places Morgan had marked and comparing them to the sheets on the table. He'd even reorganized the fucking order of the lines on the last couple poems. They should've noticed.

At least the last one was a big enough change that Morgan had finally picked up on it.

"Waterman's going to fire all of us," Luke grumbled. Him first, probably. He was second in command, after all. It was technically his fault it had taken them so damn long to see what was right in front of their faces. He'd been so distracted the past few months, putting in the hours at work and dying to get home. He wasn't going to blame this shit on Corbin, but damn, he felt like a total ass for not putting more effort into his job.

Luke decided he needed to work on balance. If he had a job left at the end of the day to balance his social life with. "This is such a fuckup. It's on me, though, I'm not going to blame you. Let me go to him."

"He's not here yet."

Luke made a face at Morgan. "Nobody's here. Not for at least two hours." He looked at the clock. "Why don't you go home and shower, and I'll do the same. Grab some breakfast, don't drink any more coffee, and then we'll go over this with the team when they get here." He sighed. "After I talk to Waterman."

Morgan nodded. "Okay. Go home and shower. Good idea."

"No more coffee," Luke repeated.

"No more coffee."

CORBIN WAS still asleep when Luke slipped into his apartment. It was so, so damn tempting to get back into bed with him and pretend the world outside his apartment didn't exist. Luke was pretty damn sure he didn't want it to exist.

He thought he'd be more excited to finally have something on NW2. He thought he'd be more excited period to do anything, even if it was fighting for his job after a colossal screwup. But he wasn't. Even with his life as he knew it possibly hanging in the balance, the only thing he seemed to think about was Corbin. Probably why he, and everyone else on his team, had missed what was right under their noses. It was frustrating as hell. Or at least it would be if he could manage to dwell on it for more than thirty seconds at a time. As it was, all he really wanted to think about was the guy sprawled starfish-style across his bed, honey gold against pale sheets.

Luke sat on the mattress and ran his hands through Corbin's hair. Corbin moaned in his sleep but rolled into Luke's touch rather than away. Seemed like they were both used to the other's presence.

"'M not tired, Mom," Corbin muttered. "There are fireworks tomorrow."

Luke tried not to laugh out loud. Instead he ruffled Corbin's hair a little harder. "Corbin, babe. I'm back."

"Luke?" Corbin opened his eyes and peered at Luke. He had tiny crow's feet at the corners when he squinted, and the freckles that had started to form across the bridge of his nose made him somehow look like a boy at the start of summer break, the kind who would be complaining to his mother about fireworks and not wanting to go to bed. Luke ruffled his hair again.

"Yup. It's me. You expecting your mother?"

"What?" Corbin made a face. "You getting back in bed?"

He chuckled. "Never mind. I'm just here for a little bit. Have to take a shower. Are you up for joining me?"

"What time is it?"

"Too early."

"Do you really have to go back to work?" Corbin asked. His smile grew from sleepy to sly.

"Unfortunately." Luke rolled his eyes at himself. "Maybe for the last time since I'm probably about to get fired. I wouldn't mind a few extra minutes with you before I do, though."

Corbin nodded and pulled the covers back. He was still naked from the night before, comfortable in his skin and gorgeously lean. Luke wanted to start all over with the touching and tasting and kissing. It killed him that they didn't have the time to really get into it the way he wanted before he went to meet his doom.

"How do you do it?" Luke asked. He'd always had to work his ass off to keep his natural love handles at bay.

"What are you talking about?" Corbin leaned over and bit lightly at the rim of Luke's ear.

"Your body. It's always so perfect."

"Like yours isn't?" Corbin scoffed and pulled Luke's Polo off. Luke had been too tired to bother with finding actual work clothes in the dark. He'd figured a pair of nicer jeans and a Polo would do until he knew what the hell he was doing there and how long he'd have to stay.

"No. Of course it's not. I've always got these." Luke pinched at his sides. "And an ass. I get that from my mother."

"Best part," Corbin said. He swatted Luke's ass, which he seemed to love. "Take off your jeans. I'll meet you in the shower."

ONE RATHER long shower and a plate full of eggs later, Luke was on his way back to the office. He didn't want to face Waterman. Nobody ever wanted to face Waterman with bad news if at all possible. Especially with the news that they'd missed something so obvious for weeks, and if it got out, it could make the department look really bad. Waterman was going to be fucking pissed, and it was his fault. If he got fired, he got fired. He had a lot in savings, and there were always private security jobs, right?

Stop. Don't deal with it until you know you have to.

He hadn't driven, which was good because his mind was all over the place. By the time he got off the train at Westminster Station, though, Luke was ready for battle. At least mostly ready. He was going to tell their boss what they'd found, take responsibility for the oversight, and let the chips fall where they may. Whatever the hell that meant. Calm. Strong. Rational. Luke strode into the office, waved at Rosie, and went right for Waterman's door. Better to get it over with than stretch out the torture of waiting.

"Luke. Come in." Waterman looked pleasant, for him, which really wasn't saying much. He didn't look openly hostile. That typically was about as good as it got. He rarely even smiled at Rosie, and she was his daughter.

"Hi, boss." Luke cleared his throat. *Don't show fear. Never show fear. Fuck, fuck, fuck.* "Morgan stumbled onto something last night. It's the NW2 case. I think we finally have a lead."

"A lead?"

"Well. Maybe more than that."

And here's where I get to tell him we've been missing the giant pink and purple polka-dotted elephant in the room for weeks. Months. Jesus.

LUKE TOOK the photocopied papers out of the folder clutched in his hand and laid them out chronologically on Waterman's desk along with Morgan's book of Covington poetry. They started with Kensington and went all the way to the one they'd found a few days before in Zurich.

Waterman gave Luke the same perplexed, impatient glance Luke had given Morgan earlier. "These are the poems he left. His calling cards. We've seen them a million times."

"They're not, though." Luke shook his head. "We didn't look at them the right way. The Nightwatchman never did anything with his poems. We checked the old crime scene photographs this morning.

They were simply poems copied word for word and typed out on a square of paper. But these are different. If we ever had a doubt that NW2 was a different person, that's totally thrown now."

Luke pointed at the first poem from Kensington and flipped to the page in the book. "See in this first one how he split the line here in half? We thought that it was just to make it fit on the page, but it wasn't." He pointed to the one from Nice. "And on this one, he actually moved these two words around. Flipped their order. We'd noticed it, but couldn't find a reason for him to have done it. Seemed more like a typo than anything. Nobody paid it much mind until Morgan saw this." Luke pointed at the Zurich paper. "See?"

"That says London?" Waterman asked. It popped out at him, just like it must've to Morgan. Maybe it was that they were from the city so the word was easier to see, maybe it was just blind luck, but there it was. Clear as day.

"Yes. And the first one says Malaga, the one after that Rome. Sir, he was telling us all along which city he'd planned to hit next. This guy is probably two jobs ahead every time. Maybe even more. I'm sure he already has the London job planned. Probably quite a bit more than that, if we're honest."

Waterman went from pensive to surprised to angry in a terrifyingly short few seconds. "You mean to tell me he's been *telling* us all along where he was going to be and not a single one of my highly trained, intelligent team members picked up on this obvious trail?"

"Um, yes." Luke didn't know what else to say.

Waterman slammed a hand down on his desk. "And is there anything else you'd like to drop on me this morning?"

"No, sir."

"Where is he going to hit in London?" Waterman growled. "It's a big city."

"That part we don't know. But if he follows his schedule, then it should happen in about two weeks. We'll have an analyst pick the poems apart to see if there's anything else in them, although I highly doubt there is. This guy's a thief, not a cryptographer."

Waterman gave him a long look. "Well, I suggest you figure it out before then. Maybe if we actually use this to catch the shit, I'll try

73

to forget that it took you half-wits this long to figure out what he's been shoving in your faces."

Luke nodded, relieved and truthfully, a little shocked. He'd expected a hell of a lot worse than an eye roll and a barbed comment. He'd have to thank Rosie for whatever she'd put in her father's tea that morning.

"And next time?" Waterman said as Luke was about to walk out of the room. "Let's not let our preconceptions ruin our vision. This isn't the same man. Don't expect him to act like the first one in any way. Figure out who he's going to hit. We'll need to beat him to it."

"Yes, sir. We're on it."

"Tell Morgan good work. At least someone's doing what they're supposed to be doing. Their *job*."

Another dig. Luke knew Waterman had noticed his mental absence lately. He was sure the whole team had. He couldn't afford to do it anymore. He needed to find NW2's London hit before it happened. If he'd read Waterman's veiled comments correctly, his job was most likely on the line.

CORBIN KNEW he'd made a huge mistake. He'd made a lot of them that spring, probably more than the rest of his professional life combined, but the newest one? It was huge. When Morgan had called in the middle of the night, well, it wouldn't have been for something small and it sure as hell had to do with him. Corbin had heard the word NW2 through the speaker when Morgan had gotten a little too excited and raised his voice. He knew that's why they'd called Luke. It had to do with him.

They'd probably figured out his cipher. Like it was that hard. Corbin remembered early spring when he'd decided to do it. Just the poems or leaving the watches like his dad hadn't been enough to excite him. He'd had to leave them little clues too. Corbin had wanted to play with Interpol. He'd wanted to watch them from a distance while he dangled himself at them and they never found him. It wasn't much fun if they never figured out what city he was going to be in until he was long gone. So he'd left them a clue. He couldn't believe it had taken them so damn long to figure it out. But they had. That meant they knew his next job was right here in London.

Usually that would make the game a tiny bit more exciting. But usually it wasn't Luke on the other end of that game. Luke was different. He was smart. He'd be able to take the city and actually *do* something with it. He should've stopped giving them clues. He should've stopped pretending to be his father. He should've done a lot of things.

Luke had been in the office for hours. It was way past lunch, and he'd left that morning after only a brief shower and a few kisses. Corbin didn't have much to do, hanging around Luke's place with only his phone and some extra clothes, but he was too uneasy to leave and go home, wait there for Luke to call, and tell him what Corbin already knew—why he'd been called in the middle of the night. No, it was best to wait where he was. But he needed something to *do*. Idleness wasn't good for him, especially when he was nervous.

Corbin wasn't a TV watcher, so that was out. Sometimes he liked to pick apart heist movies, dissect all the shit they'd done wrong that would easily get them caught, but he wasn't in the mood for that kind of entertainment. All it would do was make him more nervous.

He figured he'd go to the market and get some things to make dinner. It would keep him busy and moving. He needed to move. Cooking was something Corbin had become acquainted with over the years. He'd lived so many places in his adult life with food he didn't like, it had become a necessity at first and then a pleasure. And it wasn't something he'd done for Luke many times. So cooking it was.

He dressed and headed to the closest farmer's market. They popped up all over the city in the spring and summer months. It was something predictable about living in large cities, and Corbin loved it. Some quick research sent him on his way to the nearest market to grab things for dinner. He wished he'd gone out over the weekend to get fresh produce when there were twice as many stalls and merchants, but he'd make do with what he could find. Being picky would be another distraction from thinking about what Luke was probably doing anyway.

What's wrong with you?

In the past, Corbin would've loved the thought that they were all in that office talking about him, trying to figure out his next move, maybe getting a little closer but not close enough to really do anything. Not anymore. Not in this case. The thought made his skin crawl.

Right. To the shops.

HE WAS in the kitchen happily distracted from his worries by cooking when his phone rang. He thought it was Luke at first since he hadn't managed to bother giving people separate ring tones, but no. It most definitely wasn't Luke.

"Mother," Corbin said warily when he picked up the phone. "Can this wait? I'm making dinner."

"I see you've chosen to ignore my advice to leave London. I can't say I'm shocked."

Apparently it couldn't wait. Corbin laughed softly. "I'd be shocked if you were shocked."

He hadn't talked to his family much since he'd started seeing Luke. Especially not after, well, everything he'd learned. He didn't know how to hide it from them, and he sure as hell didn't know how to tell them he was practically living with the Interpol agent tasked with hunting him down. Even for them, that kind of game was an impossible level of complication. Corbin thought his brother might find some twisted humor in it. His mother, on the other hand, surely would not.

"I'm fine, Mother," he said. "Everything's under control."

"I'm better at reading your voice than that." She waited for him to elaborate for a few brief seconds, but when he didn't she added, "You're not fine."

"I've only said twenty words tops. How on earth could you possibly read anything?"

"You sound flushed."

"I'm cooking dinner. I was in the middle of chopping when you called. It's hot in here." *Too many details. Stop talking.*

"What are you making?" she asked.

"Pasta primavera. Why?" *And that sounded defensive.* Shit. If there was one thing his mother was better at than stealing, it was reading people and using it to her advantage. She wasn't above doing it to her children if need be.

"Who are you making it for?"

Corbin knew better than to lie outright. His mother was far too good to buy bullshit of that level. Even over the phone. "I've been seeing this guy. I'm making him dinner."

"Where did you meet him?"

"Just at a pub," Corbin tried not to sound wary.

"What does he do?"

And here's where the shit starts. "He's a banker. Works with foreign investors." Fuck. He'd said too much.

"Corbin, you fool. He's no more a banker than you are an alarm specialist." He choked. He knew she was good but damn, that was *good.* Still, he'd expected it. "Foreign clients? Lots of plane trips? What organization does he work for?"

"Mother, you're way off-base here." Corbin wanted to hang up before she made him spill everything.

"No. I'm not. Tell me what you know, darling. I'll find out anyway."

"He's Interpol," Corbin whispered. "He's American." *And he lost. That easily.*

"Oh, Jesus Christ. And I'm guessing by the fact that he's not in Manchester, he works for the London satellite office? Art crimes and high profile thefts?"

"Yes, he does, um, work in that division."

If it was possible to feel someone's pulse over the phone, then his mother's was about to skyrocket through the roof.

"Corbin, how on earth do you think you're going to get away with that? That's pure stupidity. You need to get on a plane and come home immediately."

At that point, when he was about to hang up, not that it would do a damn bit of good, another phone was picked up. "What are you doing over there? I was watching the backchannel chatter this morning and saw your little trick with the poems and the clues. Do you enjoy prison?"

"Hi, Dad. Nice to talk to you." Corbin hadn't spoken to his father in months. Usually his mom did the communicating for both of them. Corbin and good old Dad hadn't really seen eye to eye about anything in years. It probably drove his father to the point of insanity to have Corbin following his MO and messing it up.

"I heard your mom's blood pressure going up from across the garden. What have you done?" he repeated.

"He's seeing a government agent," Corbin's mother said. She wasn't one to pull punches. "It's getting serious."

"Are you out of your ever-loving mind?" His father rarely squawked. It was beneath him, Corbin supposed. He was proud to have pulled it out of him. "That game is far too dangerous. You're going to get yourself caught."

"I'm not. I'm going to stop." He'd said it just like that. They hadn't caught him, and if he didn't do anything else, they never would. Easy as that.

"What do you mean?" his father asked.

Yes, he'd quit. That was the perfect plan. Really, they didn't know much. Only that he'd planned to hit London, but Luke knew him, it seemed too close, too easy. And Luke was good. Smart. Corbin had respect for him and his position he'd never had before. So he'd stop.

"I'm not going to do the next job. I'm going to lie low and pretend to install security systems until this blows over. They'll file the case away as cold, and I'll move on."

"Away from the Interpol agent."

"His name is Luke."

There was a long pause on the line. "Luke Eldridge?" He'd managed to get another squawk from his father.

"Yes, Father."

"You have completely lost your mind. Yasmin, we're going to have to go grab our son with a straitjacket and haul him off to the state hospital."

Corbin almost laughed. He wondered when his dad had become so dramatic in his retirement. "Dad. I'm going to stop. I have it under control." Control. He had everything under control.

"Like hell you do."

Corbin decided to end the conversation by hanging up and muting his ringer. He wanted to make dinner, and that was exactly what he was going to do.

CORBIN HADN'T ever dealt with a London summer. It was overcast and sticky and uncomfortable, and the best summer he'd ever had in his entire goddamn life. Maybe it was the near constant cloud cover or the intermittent rain that seemed to seep into things like it did when it had been cold but warm and damp instead. But probably it was Luke. Luke seemed to be everywhere. In his house, on his phone, in his mind. Corbin would've thought he'd go crazy from the near constant affection, but he loved it. Like scary loved it.

They spent evenings walking around Camden Market, Sundays on Portobello Road, went on boat tours and to farmers' markets, and he nearly nauseated himself with how much of a couple they were. Or he would have if he hadn't been so disgustingly happy. The one thing that bothered him, the one thing that kept him from being completely, perfectly content was it... It. The job that hung out there, unfinished and planned and within his reach. But Luke knew about the poems. He'd learned it weeks ago from Morgan, that morning after their dinner with Rob and Trish. Corbin was almost afraid to bring it up, afraid it would ruin picnics with Rob, Trish, and the kids. He didn't want to ruin it. He wanted that damn diamond. Most of the time he could ignore the want, the need that tapped at the back of his skull.

Most of the time.

"HEY, BABE. I thought I'd make chicken parm tonight. You want a salad or pasta to go with it?" Luke asked one night in late July.

They had every window of his apartment flung wide open and three fans running. It was still hot. Corbin felt like every piece of his clothing was sticking to him.

"Salad please," he said. "I haven't gone running all week, and I had two slices of Trish's cake last night."

Luke pinched his sides. "I like your happy roll. It's cute."

"Happy roll?"

"That's what Rob called mine. I guess it just means I'm happy. He says he gained ten pounds when he first started dating Trish."

"Oh lord. We're going to the gym tomorrow. Coconut milk and kale smoothies for breakfast, no bread for three weeks."

Luke chuckled. "I'm going with salad for dinner with the chicken. And no garlic bread."

"Yes. That would be a huge no to the garlic bread." Corbin grinned but his belly fluttered with a bit of panic.

Corbin couldn't have an extra ten pounds around his middle if he wanted to get through windows and shimmy up the sides of houses. He vowed to do extra-long runs all week. Even if he wasn't going to Lord Hughes's house for that damn diamond. Even if he wasn't even thinking of the diamond. Fuck, he was thinking about the diamond. The diamond he was most assuredly *not* going to steal.

"You wanna go to the market with me?" Luke asked. "I wanted to look at the free-range chickens, and we don't really have enough stuff left for a decent salad."

"Yes." *Anything but sitting here and thinking about it. Stop thinking about it.*

THE TRIP to the market was nice, distracting the way he needed it to be. He helped Luke pick out chicken and a bell pepper for their salad. They grabbed bottles of spring water and a carton of strawberries for dessert. Corbin loved cooking with Luke. They had their little dance in the kitchen down to an art—a thing he would've thought was annoying in the past if he pictured being in a relationship. Routines, order, the "way things were done." None of that would've appealed to him. But he loved spinning around Luke to grab a lemon and some olive oil to make dressing; he loved that Luke always dipped him for a kiss when he was about to reach for the refrigerator handle. It was their thing. He liked that they had things. Sue him.

They settled on the sofa for dinner instead of sitting out on the balcony like they had the rest of the week. It had started raining while they cooked, but it was still hot, and they'd decided to stay in and watch a movie with their dinner.

He sat on the left side of Luke's couch, his side, and cuddled up to Luke while he flicked through the menu onscreen and picked the film they'd agreed on. Corbin inhaled contentedly. He loved the way Luke smelled. It was exciting, like it had been from the beginning, but there was something familiar about it now too. Comforting. Soft and sweet and spicy and his. His. That was the important thing, he thought. Sometimes Corbin wondered if he'd spent all those years acquiring things because he'd never had anything important that was his before, like Luke was. His need for it was less than it had been before. Not exactly gone, but less. It was a start.

Don't think about the diamond.

Halfway through the movie, they'd squished down into the couch in their usual position. Corbin was sprawled on Luke's chest, and Luke had his arms around Corbin. He'd pressed a few kisses into Corbin's hair and tangled their feet together.

"You liking this movie?" Luke asked softly

"Hmmm?" Corbin hadn't been paying attention really. More Luke's arms around him and Luke's smell and the way he breathed. Yeah. Not really all that into the movie.

"It's okay."

"You have no idea what's even going on, do you?"

Corbin didn't bother to hide his indulgent smile. "Not really."

"Want to go on a quick walk and then hit the sack?" Luke asked.

"Wanna skip the walk?" Corbin countered. He tipped his head back and grinned at Luke.

"Uh, yeah. Race you there."

Corbin sprang off the couch, already laughing, and ran into their room to catapult onto the bed. "Off, off, off," he said and gestured for Luke to get rid of his clothes.

"You too. I need you naked."

"I'm glad." Corbin grinned at him. Damn, it was still fun with them. It had always been fun, and five months later, it felt like the first night. They laughed and grinned and drove each other absolutely crazy in bed, and it was perfect. Corbin tackled Luke to the comforter when he finally crawled in.

"I want you," he muttered. Luke didn't ask Corbin to top all that often, which was fine by him. He loved having Luke inside him, but sometimes he craved the heat and the tightness, and he loved watching Luke fall apart when that happened.

"Yeah. I want it too. Come here." Luke wrapped a well-muscled thigh around Corbin's hips and pulled him closer. "It just keeps getting better and better, doesn't it?" he asked. "I didn't think it could get better."

"Every day," Corbin said against his lips. "Kiss me."

"Don't want to stop."

Corbin's heart *thunked* in his chest, and he leaned over for another long, wet kiss. "Then don't."

CORBIN SHOULD'VE had an easy time falling asleep. Hell, they'd managed to wear each other out more than once in the past few hours, but for some reason he was still staring up at the dark ceiling, unable to close his eyes.

"What's up?" Luke asked.

"How'd you know I was awake?" Corbin asked.

He felt Luke shrug. "I guess I just did. You feel different when you're asleep."

"And you were still awake to feel it." Corbin turned on his side and faced Luke.

Luke nodded and cupped a hand behind Corbin's neck. He pressed a soft kiss against Corbin's lips. "Yeah. Still awake."

"So how come you can't sleep?"

"I don't know. I'm just thinking, I guess."

Somehow Corbin knew without asking, but he asked anyway. "What are you thinking about?"

"Our thief. This guy... he drives me nuts. He left all these clues, he practically followed a schedule, and then nothing. He was supposed to—shit, I probably shouldn't be telling you all of this."

Corbin forced a soft smile. "What am I gonna do? Call my mom and tell her?" He put his hand on Luke's chest. "I don't want you to get in trouble, but you can talk to me. I'm not going to tell anyone."

Luke kissed him again. "I know. I trust you. I've just never been in this position before. Having someone to talk to." He was silent for a moment, but then he went on. "It's just really frustrating, you know. We know he's going to hit London. Or he was. Right now it seems like he vanished off the face of the earth. This guy was regular. Every three weeks, nearly on the dot. It's like he planned—holy shit." Luke made an annoyed face.

"What?"

"It's just that we screwed everything up by missing those clues. It was obvious all along that NW2 has been operating on some kind of schedule. He planned his schedule around when his marks weren't going to be there. He probably had a list of what he wanted and then went in order. When certain people would be out of town or out for the night, he'd hit. It's perfect, really. And it would have been perfect for us if we'd actually fucking *noticed* the obvious clues he'd left us. It wouldn't have been that hard for us to come up with a shortlist of his potential clients and whose schedule matched his. We could've gotten him."

And it was exactly what Corbin had done. Until London. He'd let his window pass, and he wasn't planning on opening it again.

Don't think about the diamond. "So what now?" Corbin tried to look interested, but like loving partner interested, not invested in the outcome interested. He hoped he got it right.

Luke shrugged. "I don't know. I don't know if he got spooked somehow or if we got a little too close, although I don't know how that's possible. He's been telling us all along where he's going to be and nobody's caught the bastard yet. I don't know what happened."

"That's a lot of 'I don't knows.' How can you even be sure it's a guy?" Corbin asked.

"I don't think I can explain it. It's little things, a detail here and there. We thought originally it was the Nightwatchman. This guy was active in the '80s, and the FBI and Interpol had profiled him as a 'him' back then. This thief almost fits that profile, but there are differences— playful where the Watchman had been methodical, smart still but less careful, almost like it's just as much about the game as winning the prize. The Watchman wasn't like that. He was all about the prize." Luke made a face. "I'm not doing a good job of explaining myself here. I don't know how I know it's a guy. I just do. It's like I can still feel his *presence* sometimes when we're at the scene. Like he's lingering there, watching and laughing. It's a man. I know it is. And he's a smartass. A very smart smartass."

Corbin's heart fluttered, and not pleasantly. Luke was so close. He was right too. His father had been detailed and goal oriented. For Corbin it was more about the chase. The prize didn't do all that much for him, not anymore. Luke knew that. He knew him. And not just the Corbin in his bed, but the one with millions of dollars' worth of stolen goods in his safe in Notting Hill. He felt exposed and scared. It wasn't a feeling he was used to. And the weirdest part of all? He wanted to huddle close to Luke, of all people, get into his arms and have Luke make the feeling go away.

Too bad he was the one with the potential power to expose Corbin to the world. Corbin shivered.

"You okay?"

"Just got cold for a second," he lied. "I'm fine now."

How could he explain that when he'd closed his eyes, he'd seen Luke standing there with a gun pointed right at his face?

AND THEN he'd squeezed the trigger.

CHAPTER SEVEN

MAYBE IT was the heat. Whatever rumors he'd heard about chilly Mother England, the summer had turned them all into a lie. A sweltering, disgustingly hot lie. The heavy, thick, overcast sky weighed down on Corbin like some kind of anvil, made him feel like he needed to escape from something, although what, he'd never be able to say. It was a hard feeling to pin down because usually he was *happy*. He was so unnervingly, overwhelmingly happy, he didn't know what to do with himself. But still it was there. *It*. The weird, heavy, antsy feeling, pushing and pulsing and itching at the back of his brain, and he wanted to scratch it. He *needed* to scratch it.

Don't think about the diamond. Don't think about the job. Stop it.

"HEY, BABE. You ready to go?"

He hadn't heard the door open. Jesus. Corbin looked up from his laptop and slammed it shut. Shit. He should've known Luke was going to be home any minute, should've *known* that looking at a certain Lord Hughes's travel schedule, which he had no right to have, wasn't exactly something he should be doing when his fucking Interpol agent boyfriend walked through the door. Corbin had been so distracted lately, he'd been making dumb mistakes. They needed to stop. Wait, what had Luke said?

"Ready?" he asked. Were they going somewhere? Going…. Oh, damn. Trish and Rob's.

"To go to dinner? With Trish and Rob."

"Yeah. Shit, I remember now. I got carried away looking at parts for this system I'm supposed to be quoting. I'm such a moron. Give me ten minutes to shower and put something decent on, and I'll be good to go."

"That's totally fine. Can I hop in with you?"

Corbin gave Luke a huge grin and promised himself he would erase his laptop history the second he had a free moment to himself. "Of course." He wasn't going to complain about naked Luke in any circumstance, but it was convenient for him to be occupied. *Better in the shower with me than figuring out my laptop password.*

"Come on in."

THE SHOWER with Luke helped with the itchy pressure of a job undone, but Corbin's head still wasn't quite in the right place. He was… antsy. Uneasy.

"Hey, babe. You okay?" Luke asked when they were on the Tube headed for Rob and Trish's house. Plans had changed when Rob and Trish found a sitter. They were going to grab pizza at a place in their neighborhood and then get a few drinks, which was fine. Of course it was fine. Corbin honestly could've used the distraction of having the girls around, but he wasn't going to complain.

"Yeah. Why?"

"You seem really spaced out today."

"Just thinking about the job, I guess." Which wasn't a lie. He'd been thinking about the Hughes job for days. Weeks, actually. It wasn't the job. It wasn't even the diamond, although he'd wanted that particular diamond for years. Lord Hughes's stone was legendary. The Pink Panther they'd called it, for its striking color and size. Corbin wanted it in his collection, he did, but even more than that, he wanted loose ends tied. He didn't have anything else planned, but he'd done such a good job of setting that one up. It drove him nuts not to see it through.

"Is it frustrating you?"

"Hmmm?"

Luke laughed indulgently. "Is the job frustrating you?"

"Oh. Yeah, it is. I just don't have all the parts I want, and I don't know if I'm going to be able to do it. I hate dropping jobs." At least part of that statement was true.

"I can tell." Luke gave him an indulgent smile. "You know, that doesn't surprise me. You definitely seem like the kind of guy who would hate flaking out when you promised to finish something."

"You have no idea." Corbin shook his head, frustrated. He really needed to talk about something else. Anything else. "Tell me about your day."

Luke shrugged. "Well, we're on a train." He laughed a little. "I can't say too much."

"Deal with any… problem customers?" Corbin didn't want to talk about Luke's involvement in finding him, but he had to.

"Yeah. One. Nothing major."

"Your, um, worst customer?"

Luke smiled at Corbin's attempt to talk around the matter. "I think he might be gone. We haven't gotten any activity from that area in weeks. Our team thinks he might have disappeared."

Good. That's exactly what you should think. "That's exactly what you want, right?"

Luke scrunched his nose. "Yes and no. I mean, yes, it's good that he's not, um, doing what he was doing. But if he had been, maybe we could've run into him. Right now, he's a ghost." Luke looked around at that, clearly aware he might have said too much.

Corbin elbowed him and changed the subject. "So, I'm reading this book. It's about the Romanovs and the whole conspiracy. I forget who wrote it, but it's not bad."

"I thought they found Anastasia's remains and proved all of that was just stories."

"Don't ruin it for me! She lived." Corbin pretended to be annoyed, and Luke grinned and threw his arm over Corbin's shoulder. A woman gave them a look, surprised at first but then slowly melting into a smile.

That's right. Smile at us. We're adorable.

Trish had told him a few weeks ago it was impossible not to fall for their romance. They were so cute and sweet together and so obviously falling for each other. She hadn't used the word love, and neither had Corbin or Luke. Out loud. But Corbin was thinking it. As crazy and irresponsible as it was, he sure as hell was thinking it.

Sometimes he caught himself fantasizing about quitting altogether. He had far more than enough money. He didn't need to work anymore. He could have Luke and family, and everything could be easy. Until he felt that itch under his skin. Until he got tired of spending random days wandering around foreign towns on a "business trip." Until he had to go back to doing what he did best. Still, it was a fantasy. A good one.

"We're here," Luke said. It was only two stops between Luke's apartment and the station for Rob and Trish's place. Corbin was grateful. The Underground during rush hour wasn't his favorite place to be, all packed with people and smells. They wove their way out of the train and up the huge escalator to the street. Trish and Rob were waiting for them at the exit.

"Couldn't wait to get out of the house?" Luke teased.

"Millie's been on a brat tirade this week. " Trish rolled her eyes. "I threatened her within an inch of her life if she's not good for the sitter. And then I cajoled and begged and promised concert tickets. I think the second one might have worked."

"What concert are you taking them to?" Luke asked with a chuckle.

"Don't even ask. And if you're not careful, I'll tell them Uncle Luke really wants to take them instead of me. Picture lots of screaming girls. And glitter. There will be much glitter."

Luke shuddered. "I hate those things. Security nightmares, they are."

"I'm starving," Rob interrupted. "We going to go, or what?"

Trish elbowed him, then pulled Corbin close and threaded her arm through his until she was hanging on his elbow. "Walk with me," she said.

Corbin walked with Trish, letting her lead the way to the pizza place and gossiping like they'd known each other for years. It was moments like that when he wished he was like them, that he didn't have the need, the itch, the desperate pull working its way under his skin. He wished he really did install high-tech security systems. Maybe he'd learn how. It couldn't be that bad a job. Right?

AFTER DINNER and drinks, he and Luke poured themselves into a cab, better than the night bus filled with London's drunks for sure, and found their way back to Luke's apartment.

"Fun night," Luke slurred. He and Rob had participated in an uncharacteristic shot competition. Luke had won. Technically. Corbin was pretty sure it wouldn't feel like a win in the morning.

"Good thing you don't have to go in tomorrow," he teased.

"No kidding. Nobody better steal any shit tonight, I swear." Luke threw out his arm. "Thieves of Europe, stay indoors! I don't feel like dealing with you."

Corbin giggled into Luke's neck. "C'mon, drunky. Let's brush our teeth and go to bed."

"Like you can talk. How many glasses of white wine did you have?"

"Only three. I promise. Let's go to bed." Corbin was feeling wobbly and warm-bellied. He slipped his hand up under Luke's shirt.

"For fun times?" Luke asked. He had this sweet hopeful smile that made Corbin want to drag his shirt off.

"Babe, I'm so tired. You have to be tired too."

"We're married already," Luke said dramatically. "He's rejecting my advances."

"I'm not!" Corbin protested.

They laughed with each other, giggling and pulling at clothing, hip checking in the bathroom mirror and flicking each other with soap and toothpaste as they got ready for bed. It felt so damn good, so domestic and so wonderful. It nearly scratched the itch that thrummed under Corbin's skin. But it didn't.

Don't think about the diamond. Don't think about the diamond.

But he did.

Until that damn thing wasn't sitting across town calling his name, mocking his careful planning, he'd never get it out of his head, no matter how many dinners, drinks, or hot nights of sex he had with Luke. The fucking thing wasn't going to go away, and there was only one thing he could do about it.

Get the diamond.

"HEY, MA." Luke felt a little sheepish about how many calls from his family he'd missed lately. Or ignored. Mostly ignored, if he was telling the truth, and the number was pretty high. He loved his family, but he'd wanted to keep Corbin to himself as long as he could before he got his nosey parents into the whole thing. It was just like he'd felt about bringing him around to Rob and Trish. But since he'd already done that, well, it was probably a huge mistake not to call and talk to his mom about it. Trish didn't talk to Luke's parents every week, but she did quite often. Luke would never live it down if his family heard about Corbin from someone else first. They probably already had.

"Luke. I thought you might have died."

"Sorry." Okay, so there it was. He did feel guilty. Thirty-eight years old, and his mom still somehow had the power to make him feel like a misbehaving toddler. Maybe he should hire her to work in his division. Waterman might actually like her, unlike Luke. Sometimes Luke felt like Waterman was keeping him around until he screwed up just enough to fire. "I'm not dead. I've just been really busy."

"Trish told me you've been busy all right."

Too late. Shit fuck.

"Trish has a big mouth," he snapped. He and his mom were like that. They traded guilt trips and barbed remarks, but they had a great time being pissy with each other. And they loved each other more than anything. Luke often wished he could pick up his parents and sisters and move them to London. The past few years would've been better with them around.

"Trish," his mother said in a sarcastic voice, "actually knows how to use her telephone. *E-mail*: I swear it's worse than not talking at all."

Luke had e-mailed his mother a few times a week since the NW2 case started and he'd gotten crazy busy. Okay, he was lying to himself. He'd e-mailed her since he started seeing Corbin. It was easier to avoid her questions that way. Like a heat-seeking missile, she was. Impossible to avoid her when she wanted to know something. Luke figured that trait was passed down to him. Good thing.

"Okay, so yes. She's right. I'm seeing someone."

"Was it that hard to say?" she asked.

"It's new, and I really didn't want the third degree."

"Since when do I give you the third degree?"

Luke snorted hard. "Please. Scotland Yard could learn some techniques from you. Probably quite a few," he grumbled under his breath. But he didn't elaborate. His mother had already gotten more than one rant about his issues with the head of Scotland Yard. She probably didn't want to hear it again.

"So now you're going to have to tell me about him. You're aware of this, right?"

"I figured as much." And the thing was, Luke *wanted* to talk about Corbin. He wanted to talk about him all the damn time. He'd already done it with Trish and Rob, probably until they were so tired of hearing about him they wanted to scream. But it was weird to say those things to his mom. They hadn't ever really talked about his dating life—probably because he'd never had much of one, but still. It wasn't something they did. And here he was doing just that.

"So?" she prodded. "First time my son has an official boyfriend after all these years. Speak."

Jesus. Luke chuckled. "No pressure. He's really great, Ma. His name is Corbin. He's American too. Works here like I do."

"Has he been in London long?"

"No. Only a couple of months before I met him. He does security systems for big clients."

"Is 'security systems' code for CIA?"

Luke laughed out loud. He really loved his mother sometimes. "No. Pretty sure Corbin's not CIA."

"How sure?"

"I'm not going to run my boyfriend through facial recognition, Ma. I trust him." Plus he didn't have that government veneer about him. Luke could pick out an agent in a crowded room. Corbin wasn't one.

"It's the best way to know for sure."

"Maybe you should've worked for Interpol. You're better at this job than I am."

"I just want you to be safe. Tell me more about him. What's he look like?"

"I can e-mail you a picture, you know?" Luke teased.

She made an indelicate noise. "I'm sure you can. After you tell me."

"He's smaller than me. Little but wiry, pretty brown eyes, light brown hair." *Curvy and sexy and smart, and more fun than I've ever had in my life.*

"Is he good in bed?"

"I'm hanging up." Luke felt his face flame bright red. He'd have never told his mom about the nights at the pub, dragging nameless twinks home or to the bathroom for meaningless one-offs. He had no idea why she'd decided to ask about Corbin. Again, it wasn't a conversation they regularly had.

"I'm just curious."

His mom was always "just curious." "Everything's great in that department. Done talking about it."

"Oh dear. You and your sisters did come from somewhere, you know. Is he well endowed?"

"Fuck, Mom. I really am hanging up."

"No swearing." She sounded like she had when Luke was fifteen.

"I think I deserve a few swear words after you asked about my boyfriend's dick. I might die of embarrassment."

"You're a government agent. You'll get over it. So tell me, what do you see for you two?"

"I don't know. I haven't gotten there yet. I really like him. More than that, actually. We're taking it one day at a time."

"What do you mean by more?"

He hadn't even said it to himself, but he felt it, large and overwhelming, swallowing him whole. "I think I'm in love, Ma. I mean, I haven't been before, but I just... kinda knew. He feels right. *We* feel right."

"That sounds like love to me, baby." Her voice went from its usual probing acerbic curiosity to gentle. "I thought we'd be having this discussion years ago, but I'm happy for you if you think he's the right guy."

"I really do. I haven't felt like this before. I love being around him."

"Then I'm going to need to meet this one, I believe. I was planning to come visit in the fall. London is lovely in September."

Luke thought about him and Corbin in a couple of months' time, walking through a golden-hued city, showing his mother around. Corbin would charm her just like he'd charmed Trish and Rob and the girls.

"I think that's a good plan to make."

"THANK YOU for dinner. It was really good."

Corbin relaxed into Luke's bed. He'd been happier at Luke's place than anywhere he'd ever been in his life. It had been weeks since he'd been back to his own apartment other than to drop off clothes and come back. The restless niggle was still in the back of his head, the feeling of a job left undone, of stashes left to plunder, but he tried to ignore it.

"I don't have too many dishes mastered, but that one I can do with my eyes closed." Luke kneeled on the bed and leaned over Corbin to give him a long kiss. "You have to leave tomorrow, right?"

Corbin nodded. He'd manufactured a job in Paris so it wouldn't look weird that he wasn't working. It was a "big one," so he didn't have to take another trip for a long time. He figured he'd mess around in the city for a day or two, buy some clothes, and then come home to Luke. He didn't want to leave. London was beautiful in June, and all he wanted was to hang around Luke's place, go shopping, and... no. *Don't think about that damn diamond.* He'd been doing really well for the past few days, but it was nearly impossible not to think about it. Every cell in Corbin's body hated leaving a job undone. Luke's team couldn't narrow it down to a single house, could they? Especially when they didn't expect him to strike anymore.

"You want dessert?" Luke asked. "I bought gelato on the way home. Mint, like you like."

"That sounds amazing. I'll help you get it." He hauled himself up and followed Luke to the kitchen. The living room only had one lamp lit; it was soft and dark and homey. Corbin maneuvered his way around furniture and into the small updated kitchen.

"I'll get bowls out," he said.

"I love you," Luke's voice rang out, quiet but gruff in the silence of the room. "*Fuck.* I can't believe I just said that."

Corbin's hand shook where it rested on the cabinet knob. "Did you mean it?" he asked.

"Yes. I mean, Jesus. I don't have much experience with this. I don't have *any* experience with this, but yeah. I mean it. I didn't mean to say it, but I meant it. I know you're still skittish, and we weren't planning to be serious but—"

Corbin held a hand over Luke's mouth. "I love you too."

He was terrified of what he'd just said. Here he was with the guy who literally had the ability to fuck Corbin's future in every possible way. He was dangerous and so very not on Corbin's side of the law, but every cell in Corbin's body told him to step closer. Every hair on his skin told him to take the gelato container out of Luke's hand and twine their fingers together. The stars floating in his blood must've tilted his head back and made him brush a soft kiss over Luke's lips. But only he could take credit for what he did next.

"I love you." Corbin whispered it again in case Luke hadn't heard it the first time. "I love you." Luke wrapped his hand around Corbin's neck and hauled him into a deep, hard kiss. It lasted for nearly a breathless minute before they drew apart, grinning at each other.

"I thought I'd fucked everything up for a second there," Luke confessed.

"I'm not a dickhead."

"You would've let me down easy?" Luke chuckled.

It was shaky, kind of like how Corbin's insides felt. He could scale a wall on a rope, had the fingers and the nerves to unlock complex safes, and escape from tall buildings with priceless treasures, but one love confession from what should've been the wrong man made his knees turn to warm soup.

He clutched at Luke's arm. "So, we're kind of stuck with each other for a while?"

"I think I'd like that," Luke said. "And just in case I wasn't clear enough the last time, I love you too. I like...." He trailed off and blushed. "I never want to leave when I'm with you. I hate when you leave too. You're an addiction."

"I know how you feel." Corbin ran his fingers up Luke's chest and around the back of his neck. He pulled Luke in for another kiss, this one soft and only lingering for a few brief seconds. "I don't want to go either."

"Do you still want gelato?" Luke asked.

Corbin giggled against his lips. "You really going to offer me dessert and then do take-backs? Yes, we need gelato. We need to celebrate."

"I can think of another way to do that," Luke said. His expression was so serious Corbin had to laugh again. Of course he could.

"Why don't we scoop some of this out and take it to bed. Maybe we can celebrate twice. Hell, it'll take me a few minutes to get over feeling like an awkward teenager, and sugar can only help."

Luke tickled him. "You're not awkward. You're sexy."

"Oh my god. Give me a spoon before we injure ourselves trying to express emotion."

They teased each other through spooning out gelato, and Corbin chased Luke back to bed. They finished their ice cream and then dove under the covers to celebrate again, all touches and bare skin and laughter. Later, when Luke was asleep and Corbin lay drowsing and nearly there, he decided he could forget about Hughes's diamond for a little while. He didn't need that shit anymore. He had plenty of money, and he had love, something ingrained in him to avoid but the exact thing he all of a sudden couldn't live without. Corbin snuggled a bit more under Luke's light summer duvet, wrapped his arms around Luke's belly, and fell asleep cuddled up to miles of warm bronze skin.

IF THERE was anything Luke didn't want after the night he'd had with Corbin, it was to be stuck in a windowless room with Morgan discussing NW2. Again. Yes, Waterman had made it very clear that he'd better fucking find him, and he'd made it very clear it had to be before their thief struck again, but the guy wasn't striking. He should've stolen whatever he was going to steal in London nearly a month ago, and it hadn't happened. Luke wanted nothing to do with it. Sure he was curious, but he wanted to get his cases done for the day and go home and be in love. Sprawl on the couch and hang out with Corbin and not be the same guy he'd been for way too long. He didn't want a case to consume him—any case. He was tired of that life.

It was so tempting to tell Morgan to deal with everything and take off. But he needed his damn job. There weren't a lot of options open to him in London, and for the first time in years, he wasn't partly considering moving home. Not anymore at least.

"We're getting a profiler in today," Morgan said.

"Hmm?"

"Headquarters. They've flown someone out for the week. Supposed to be some sort of prodigy. She's going to help us build a profile. Narrow down where this guy's going to hit next."

"I'm not sure he's *going* to hit again. Something happened, Morgan. His game is off or something. Maybe he got caught. He's not following his pattern."

"Let's see what Baker thinks."

"That the profiler?"

"Yeah. She's supposed to be here any minute."

Luke sank down into a chair and waited, and not very patiently at that. He didn't have any problems with the woman; he'd definitely listen to what she had to say. He just didn't want to deal with it. For the first time in his life, his job wasn't the most important thing to him. Even after the wake-up call with NW2 and Waterman's barely veiled threats. He still didn't give a shit. It was just a few diamonds, right? A painting here and there. Some emeralds. Nobody was getting hurt. Corbin was making salmon and garlic mashed potatoes for dinner. That's what Luke really wanted to think about. He barely recognized himself, but after a lifetime of being his job, he didn't even think it was a bad thing to finally be someone else.

THAT WAS the moment when the office door swung open and Ariana Baker came striding in. Everything about her said efficient, from her very official suit to her very official ponytail and the demeanor that said she could take over the world. Morgan stuck out his hand and introduced himself. She replied politely. Luke rose to introduce himself as well.

"Agent Eldridge," she said. "It's a pleasure. I've heard so much about you. I can't believe I'm meeting you in person. We studied a few of your cases when I was in training." She had a light accent. German, Luke thought.

"Jesus, I feel old."

Baker giggled. If he wasn't wrong, she was flirting with him. Fantastic. The next thing would be her asking him to show her a great place for dinner in the city, and there was no way he was getting involved in any of that, work or not. He was going to listen to her, get some ideas on a case he was pretty sure had gone cold, and then go the hell home to his boyfriend.

"I studied the files you have on NW2 on the way over here. I had plenty of time."

Luke shrugged. "Anything we have is yours. I don't know if you're going to get much more out of what we have, but you're welcome to give it a try."

"No, this will be great. It's pretty simple. I think I can narrow it down to a few types. Some people he might be interested in. From there, maybe we can get some specific people. I don't know the possible victim pool here as well as you folks do."

"By all means." Luke gestured. "Let me grab Kelly, and you have the floor."

Rob, lucky bastard, was out for the day. Luke only wished he was too. If he'd been able to come up with a reason he needed to see Tessa's school play, than he'd have been there in a heartbeat. They waited while Kelly got into the room and settled, then Baker opened up a new file on the SMARTboard.

"Here's what we have," she said. "This guy likes gems. That's for sure."

"But he's gone after paintings too. And a few relics. Artifacts."

She nodded. "Yes, we've noticed that, but there's a different quality to those jobs. Like it's more about function and less about... love. We can guess that he'd go after one of those pieces, but he's done two in a row. He's going to be drawn to a gem this time. He misses them."

That did make sense. "So, gems. You think he's going to go for a gem again."

"Yes. Large, unusual, famous, privately owned gems. Something flashy. I know there's money in this city, but the list of what we're looking for can't be that long."

"We've been compiling it ever since we found the clues in the poems. It's not done yet, but I'll hand over what we have so far. If you're sure it's going to be a jewel, we can filter out the names of people who don't own anything substantial in that department."

"That would be fantastic if you could do that. From there, it'll be easy. He likes a challenge. If it's too easy, it's not fun. He probably doesn't need any money at this point. It'd be more about the personal meaning, the prestige. He'll want something he can feel good about having gotten. Something... worth his while."

"You think he's going to go private, though? Not like a museum?" If NW2 was going for a challenge, he'd hit more than enough houses. The original liked to escalate when he got bored. Perhaps his successor was the same.

"There's nothing here that makes me think he's going to go that high profile. It's too difficult. He's smart, and he likes to take risks, but he's not reckless. Stay private. Go for decent security but not too good. Maybe people who are very public. Ones who have a schedule that's easy to access. People who leave town more often than not. Those are the ones he'll target. Those are the ones he can get to."

"Big noteworthy gems, medium security, still a challenge but not stupid. Out of town, public person."

"Yes. You shouldn't have too long of a list if you combine all those things."

"You'd be surprised."

"Well, it'll be a starting place."

"I can work on that," Morgan said. Luke thought his face might have twitched for a second, like the profiler made him nervous. Luke didn't blame him. She looked at all of them like she was measuring them. It was unnerving to say the least.

CORBIN SHOULD'VE known. There had to be some sort of cosmic warning, something telling him that no, it really wasn't a good idea to finish the job. Thinking back, there'd probably been more than one warning.

But he had to do it. It had gotten to the point where it was the only thing he could think about, finishing what he'd started. So he took a "trip" and went to his apartment, which was far enough away from Luke's so he could plan in peace. Luke thought he was out of the country and made a cute puppy face and told him not to stay away long. Corbin felt like a dick but made sure to text Luke as often as he could.

He got lucky somehow. The Earl was gone again according to the agenda his assistant kept in a not very well secured file on his computer. It hadn't taken Corbin much effort to get into it the first time, and it took no effort at all for him to get back into it again. He had free time that weekend.

Shit. Too quick. I can't do that.

Corbin liked to plan. He liked weeks to set everything up and make sure he was in the clear. But the schedule was tight; Hughes wasn't going to be out of town again for nearly a month. He didn't know if he could stand to wait that long, and he didn't have the time or the concentration to set up a whole new job. It had to be the Pink Panther, it had to be him, and apparently it had to be that weekend.

He called Luke. It made his stomach coil to lie outright once again, but he wouldn't have to anymore after the job was done.

"Hey, babe."

"You on your way back?" Luke's voice sounded hopeful and happy and loving.

Corbin dug his nails into his palm. They'd planned to make cookies that weekend and veg out in front of Luke's TV with a whole season of something cheesy. It had been an awesome plan, one he'd been on board with until it seemed like his only window to get the Pink Panther was a hell of a lot closer than it had seemed. "No, I'm not."

"Oh, really? You liking being back in the States a little too much?" Luke asked. "Don't tell me you ran away with a surfer in Miami."

"Yes. That's exactly it." Corbin chuckled despite himself. "Actually, I'm here right now with someone else... this whole roll of blueprints that I've run away with. It's hot. It's so hot."

Luke chuckled. "Job giving you trouble?"

"Yeah. I think I'm going to have to stay through the weekend to get this all planned out. I'm sorry."

"It's okay. I'll just have to watch *Pretty Little Liars* with my other boyfriend. He's really more into oil massages, though. So maybe I'll wait for you."

"You better! I don't want to miss out on the beginning of season three. Tell your other boyfriend he's going to have to stick to sex. No TV. That's my domain."

Luke snorted. "My other boyfriend is honestly going to be Waterman this weekend, I think. I probably wasn't going to get much free time either."

"He breathing down your ass?"

"As usual. He's got me in here profiling with someone from headquarters. I haven't done this since my days at the FBI academy."

"Oooh, profiling. That sounds sexy. Are you going to be Sherlock by the time I get back?"

"Totally. I didn't know you had a thing for Sherlock."

"Everyone has a thing for Sherlock. I'll be your Watson. I totally think there's something going on between those two."

Luke chuckled again. "Doesn't everybody?"

"Hey," Corbin said quietly.

"Yeah?"

"I'm gonna miss you this weekend. I really do wish I was at home."

"Me too. Work's lame. We should rob a bank and become millionaires."

Corbin swallowed. *That's a little awkward.* "Lemme know when you want to become outlaws on the lam."

"I love you," Luke said.

"I love you too. Be safe, and I'll see you Sunday night?"

"Yeah. Probably. You be safe too."

They hung up, and Corbin sank back onto a couch that was nowhere near as comfortable as Luke's. He was in it. Too late to back out.

AND THAT'S how, at three in the morning on Sunday, when it was still cool and overcast, Corbin crept into Lord Hughes's master bedroom and into the wardrobe where he kept his safe. Where he kept the Pink Panther. Corbin needed to get in, get out, and get the hell on the way. Then he could go back to Luke and forget about—

Don't think about Luke not right now.

Luke was his biggest distraction. One he couldn't afford.

THERE WAS something weird in the air. He didn't know if it was the already opened window, cracked just a few inches when Hughes usually kept his house bolted shut, the rank stale smell or something else, but it didn't seem right. Usually it would've been enough for Corbin to abort, but he wanted to get the damn job over with so he could forget about it and go about the rest of his life—hopefully in peace.

He focused his flashlight on the wardrobe. Tried to keep his mind on the job. It was usually so easy for him. He nearly always had tunnel vision. Not that night. Corbin should've left. He should've turned around when he couldn't stop thinking about Luke, should've given up and climbed back out the window when something in the room didn't feel right. But he didn't. His need to finish what he'd started made him stay and crack open the wardrobe to start working on the safe. Of course it did. He couldn't resist.

That's why he was still there with his hands deep in the safe when the door burst open and lights flooded the room. All of a sudden, he was swarmed by uniformed officers, frozen in place. They surrounded him in a blur. He didn't know what to think or feel. It was all a bit numb, really. They handcuffed him to a table, forced him to sit on the ground. It didn't even register.

He'd been caught.

That wasn't all. Corbin had known something was wrong, something was off, but he didn't know what until he looked at the bed. There was a small spatter of blood on the pale fabric headboard and a body sprawled across an expensive silk duvet. Corbin couldn't see much from his vantage point on the floor, but it was enough to make him nearly gag. There was a dead body in the room. A dead fucking body. He'd been found in the room with a stiff, and they were—he leaned over and puked all over the expensive Persian rug. It wasn't until he sat up, wiping the vomit from his mouth, that he saw him.

Luke.

Luke was standing in the doorway of Lord Hughes's bedroom staring at him.

Fuck.

CHAPTER EIGHT

HE WAS in shock. That was the only possible reason why Corbin couldn't move a single muscle in his body. Luke stood there staring at him, hard and long and so fucking hurt, like he was having a hard time breathing. Corbin got it. It was nearly impossible for him to drag breath into his protesting lungs as well. It felt like his body was collapsing inward. Corbin shouted in his head, ran for Luke, hugged him, kissed him, told him it really, really wasn't what it looked like, and he wasn't lying about his feelings. Every part of them was real, and he hadn't *killed* anybody.

He did all that in his head.

But in reality he didn't move, didn't say a word, just sat there cuffed to a table while he watched them move the tall, lanky—how the hell could he have missed it?—dead body of Lord Hughes out of the room.

How could I have been so stupid?

Every part of him knew it had been a bad idea. Every part of him knew he should've dropped the damn heist and never looked back. He'd felt it in his bones underneath the itch that had pushed him forward. If he hadn't been so stupid, he could be waiting in Luke's bed at this exact moment or in there with him since Luke would've never been called if Corbin wasn't here. Instead, he was cuffed in the middle of a swarm of London police with the only man he'd ever loved in his life staring at him like he was a murderer.

"You're coming with us," a gruff voice said.

His cuff was removed, and he was yanked to his feet, where his arms were fastened behind him once again. It was rough, and it *hurt*. Corbin wanted to cry out, but his pride kept him silent. He tripped on the vomit-stained Persian rug and nearly fell to his knees, but he managed to keep walking. When he saw the body on the bed staring lifelessly at the ceiling, he nearly vomited again. It was horrifying that someone would do that to a person, even worse that they thought he would. *I didn't do this. I could never do this.*

"Luke," he whispered as he walked by him, trying to put everything he was thinking in that one word, but Luke averted his eyes. He refused to look Corbin in the face. It hurt like bloody hell, a hell of a lot worse than the handcuffs digging into his skin. He shouldn't be surprised. He wasn't surprised. Hell, Luke probably thought he was a murderer on top of finding out he was a thief. He'd be lucky if he ever saw Luke again. Or daylight.

Corbin had to do something. It was one thing going to jail for something he'd actually done, but if they were arresting him for *murder*? He refused to let anyone think he was capable of that. Except as far as he could tell, they did. He had to find a way to convince them he would never do that.

"I didn't kill anyone," he protested as they led him toward the staircase. "I'm not a murderer."

"We'll see about that down at headquarters," the policeman said roughly.

He was dragged out of Hughes's house and thrown into the back of a police car. His out-of-condition shoulders ached from his climb to the second story window, and it was starting to hurt to have them fastened behind him. Add that to the wrists and his broken heart. Everything hurt, and all of it was 100 percent his fault. He should've listened to his mother. He should've listened to his gut. Corbin went to move and a sharp pain sliced down his arm from where his shoulder was bent unnaturally.

"Can you uncuff me?" he asked the officer, who was about to start the car. "I won't go anywhere."

"Not bloody likely. If you can climb into a window to kill someone—"

"I *didn't* kill anyone."

"Enough. If you can climb up the side of a house, you can easily get away from this car. No more out of you. I want quiet."

IT WAS silent the rest of the way to police headquarters. He didn't have anything to say, and he sure as hell wasn't going to incriminate himself any further if he didn't have to. He wasn't the killer. They'd have to be able to figure that out somehow. Corbin would never kill anyone. The thought of it made his insides crawl. The car wound its way through London, still dark and silent, to the building Corbin had hoped he'd never see the inside of.

Scotland Yard, or New Scotland Yard officially, was tall with slick glass sides. Dark and foreboding in the heart of the night. He didn't see a way out of there that would go in his favor. They parked behind the building, and the door opened. Corbin tried to get out on his own, but it wasn't easy, and he nearly fell again.

"Some cat burglar you are," the officer said. His voice was gruff and low. Angry. Corbin didn't blame him. "Least we caught you before you killed anyone else."

"I said I'm not a killer," Corbin repeated. "I would *never*."

"I'm taking you to lockup. You'll get to talk to Director Clarke when he gets in."

Corbin recognized that name. He'd not been one of Luke's favorite people. They clashed regularly, along with a few of his detectives, from what Corbin remembered of Luke's stories. At least he wasn't a complete unknown. According to Luke, he was arrogant and full of himself, he hated to lose, and he hated other people getting in on his territory. Corbin knew how to handle men like that—if he got the chance to explain himself in person, that was.

He was led to a cell and uncuffed. The officer looked at him like he didn't trust that the cell would be able to keep him. Given enough time and a few easy-to-make tools, he was probably right, but Corbin had decided it was probably good to stay on his best behavior.

Corbin sat. He sat, and he waited.

A LITTLE while later, he was brought out and processed. His fingerprints were taken, which made him cringe the entire time. He was officially in the system. He'd never be anonymous anymore, that was for sure—if he managed to get out of the mess he was in. How the hell could he get out of it? There didn't seem to be very many options.

Corbin was booked and put back into the holding cell, where he sat alone in the dark and waited for who knows how long to hear his fate, at least his immediate fate. He probably had months of hell ahead of him. A while later, hours maybe, after he'd been given a plastic bottle of water and a dry sandwich, a man came to his cell.

Clarke.

He wore a suit, but it didn't fit him like Luke's always did. He was tall and broad-shouldered, had salt and pepper hair, and was arrogant. Lord, was he arrogant. It only took Corbin moments to figure out why Luke despised him and half of his detectives so much.

"You're not the gunman" was how Clarke opened.

"I know. I didn't kill anybody. But...." Corbin had been about to defend himself, but how had they—"Wait, you said I wasn't the gunman?"

"Lord Hughes was shot at point-blank range between seven and nine p.m. according to our medical examiner. You don't have any gunpowder residue on your hands or your gloves and that time of death would've placed you at the crime scene for hours. While it was only drizzling lightly the whole time, your footprints were fresh in the ground outside. They would have been partially washed away if you'd been at the scene when Hughes was shot. The facts don't add up, and we can't hold you for the murder with a complete lack of evidence."

Relief fled through Corbin's body. "I was in Notting Hill during your window. I went to a corner store. They have security cameras. You'll be able to see my face."

It was something that had always bothered him before, that at any given time he could be on camera, recorded for the world to see. But he had no problems using it in this case. Hell, if it backed up Clarke's convictions that he wasn't the killer, he'd kiss the damn security cameras.

"We'll need to get an address from you to corroborate, just to be safe."

"Yes. Of course."

"And Lord Hughes. If you weren't at his house to kill him, why were you there?"

Corbin suddenly understood Luke's derision toward the Metropolitan Police. "Isn't it obvious? I'm a thief. I believe you called Interpol to the scene for a reason."

"They were already there." Clarke made a face. "How could you possibly not notice a dead body lying in the middle of the room?"

"It was dark. I knew something was wrong, I could feel it, I could even smell it, but I wanted to finish my job and get out of there. I... just knew something was wrong. I don't have any explanation for it. I studied Hughes for months, but things weren't as planned. I should've left."

Corbin slammed his lips shut. *Quit talking. What's wrong with you?*

"I'm going to turn you over to Interpol. They seemed quite interested in the contents of your bag. According to Waterman, you're their problem now, and I don't have time for you. I might need you to give a statement, but you're no longer a suspect of Scotland Yard."

"Y-You're going to give me to Interpol?" Luke. They were giving him to Luke. Corbin was both relieved and terrified. He'd lost his cool for a moment in front of Clarke, but he didn't care. He wasn't a murder suspect, and he was going to see Luke. Somehow, some way, it was going to work out.

"They're sending a driver for you now. He should be here in minutes."

"Just like that?"

"We have a murder to solve. You're wasting our time. Your case is Interpol's jurisdiction, not mine. I have enough to deal with without you making it worse."

All right, then.

Clarke turned on his heel and walked away. Just like that, he'd been cleared of the murder he had in no way committed, but he was still so very screwed. Interpol was coming for him. Luke was coming for him. Maybe he hadn't killed anyone but just the few things they knew he'd stolen in the last few months could get him put away for the rest of his life.

SMASH.

It helped to throw things: his graduation certificate, an empty coffee cup, his cell phone. One by one they crashed into the wall of his office. Luke knew the others probably thought he was insane for the way he was reacting. He didn't give a fuck. Corbin. How the hell could he? How could he look Luke in the eye and lie like that, tell him he was in love, tell him they were forever?

Actually he'd never said that, Luke reasoned. He sure as fucking hell had implied it, though. Implied they had a real chance to be something, Luke's first real chance ever. He had to get angry, had to throw things. If he didn't, nothing would stop the hurt from ripping through him, tearing little pieces out of his skin and belly and muscles until he was a bleeding mass dissolved on the floor. So he threw the vase that held the dahlias he and Corbin had picked out at the market only two days ago, and the framed photograph of his parents, and the cup that held his pens.

Smash, smash, smash.

He felt better for a moment. Until he thought of Corbin again, and it all went back to shit.

His desk phone rang. Luke didn't want to pick it up, but he was at work. He couldn't avoid reality. "What?" he barked.

"I need you in my office." Waterman.

Well, at least someone was going to be happy. They had gotten their guy. NW2 was caught. Too bad Luke's entire life had come crashing down with it. He doubted Waterman cared.

"What is it, Waterman?" Luke asked when he got to his boss' office. He hadn't used that tone before, not with someone he was truthfully a little afraid of. But apparently the time had come for Luke to snap. He didn't give a shit about his job. He didn't give a shit about anything. He needed to throw something else very, very soon.

"You might want to check your tone with me, young man." Waterman gave him a long look, then dismissed his irritation. "We have NW2 in custody. Scotland Yard released him to us, and we're going to have to decide who to turn him in to. The list is long. He's wanted in multiple countries."

They had Corbin. They had—

"Why is he here?" Luke didn't understand. There had been blood. So much blood.

Waterman made a face. "He's been cleared of the murder. He's ours to deal with."

"Cleared. He... he didn't?" Luke was stunned into silence after that. Corbin hadn't killed Hughes. He had stolen, over and over and over, and lied to Luke about everything, but at least he wasn't a killer. Luke felt like throwing up.

"He wasn't anywhere near Hughes's house during the window the ME gave for the shooting. He did, however, attempt to steal a rather large diamond from Lord Hughes and he had two very interesting items in his bag. I'm sure you already know the rest. We're going to have to figure out what to do with him. Probably have him extradited to the States for trial. He's wanted there, too, for similar thefts. Popular boy."

Waterman's ironic eyebrows rose again. Sometimes Luke wanted to reach across the desk and rip them out. It was one of those times. They were going to take Corbin to the States to punish him. Take him home. A huge part of Luke protested at that. He wanted to punish Corbin himself. Make him pay for letting Luke fall for him and turn himself into the biggest fool alive. Some latent part of him still wanted to curl Corbin up in his arms and protect him. Luke wondered when that instinct would finally die. Soon would be fantastic.

"Is there anything else?" he asked Waterman. "As you can imagine, I have a rather large pile of paperwork in my office. If what you've told me is true, then it just got significantly larger."

"That's all. I'll call you when I've decided how to proceed. I have some phone calls to make."

Luke nodded tightly and stood. "Thank you for letting me know."

He was about to walk out the door when Waterman stopped him. "Luke."

"Yes?"

"I know. I know what Corbin Ford meant to you. You didn't...."

"Are you asking me if I knew who he was?" Luke ground out. He wanted to slice things in half. Smash them to tiny little pieces.

"I suppose I'm not. Your face tells me what I need to know." Waterman gave him a curt nod.

"It should've never been a question. Of course I had no idea."

He strode from the office, probably for the last time since he was definitely getting fired for being such an ass to his boss, and stalked to his own office, where he could do some more damage.

"Hey. Luke."

Rob had just gotten in, but it was clear from his face he knew exactly what had happened.

"Man, you look like hell. Are you okay?"

"Yeah. I'm fine." Luke answered tersely. He had to be fine. He'd deal with all of this until they shipped Corbin out of his fucking sight, and he forgot that one summer he'd been a fool and fell for the wrong man.

"You don't look fine. I'm really sorry. I don't even know what to say."

Luke laughed. It sounded shitty even to him. "What, they don't make a card for that? Sorry your new boyfriend is secretly an internationally famous thief. Here's a cake." He laughed again at his own joke.

Rob gave him a pitying look. "Why don't you go home and shower. You've been here all night. Kelly told me."

"Shower? How... I can't. No. I need to be here." How could he go home and get in the shower where Corbin's shampoo was perched on the rim of the tub, brush his teeth when Corbin's toothbrush was in the cup right next to his, grab a shirt from the—no. Not going home. "I can't. I need to be here right now."

"You need to sleep."

"How the fuck am I gonna sleep, Rob? How? Would you sleep well in the bed you shared with Trish if it was *her* in that holding cell?"

"No. You're right. Maybe...." Rob took a long breath. "Maybe you need to talk to Corbin."

"Yes. That's exactly what I need." *What I really need is to get as far away from anywhere I ever stood with him so I can forget he once existed.* Luke didn't even know if that was possible and if it was, he didn't know if he wanted it. But he didn't want to talk to him. He couldn't.

"I think you might need to," Rob said. "I think, for your peace of mind, you need to see what happened. You need to hear what he has to say."

"Why?" Luke asked. He gave Rob a cheerless smile. "Even if he tells me, it'll probably be all lies anyway. There's no point."

"You don't know that. Go talk to him. You'll feel better if you do."

IT TOOK him a long time, but he did it. He made his way back to their rather informal holding cell where... *shit.* Where Corbin was sitting, waiting to see what they were going to do with him. Corbin. Luke still couldn't wrap his head around it, as much as he'd seen, as much as he'd tried to let it sink in. It was like he didn't want it to sink in. Corbin wasn't supposed to be there. Luke wasn't supposed to be angry. None of it was supposed to be so fucked.

It was dark in the holding area, and cold. He shivered even in his suit jacket. Corbin was sitting in the cell on a bench. He looked like he was half-asleep, but Luke knew he wasn't. Corbin didn't look like that when he was really sleeping. That was the weird and awful part of all this. He knew Corbin, knew him down to his bones, or so he'd thought. Luke let himself into the cell and sank into the chair across from Corbin's bench. He just stared for a long time. At first Corbin wouldn't meet his eyes, but then he did. He stared right back. He looked sorry, if that's what that expression was. Like he didn't mean to do what he'd done. Hadn't meant to fuck everything up. Fuck *them* up.

"I trusted you," Luke finally said quietly. "I loved you."

"Loved?" Corbin asked quietly, like that was the only thing he could hear.

"Yes."

"I wasn't ever going to hurt you. I wasn't going to hurt anyone. You know that."

"You swear you didn't kill Hughes?"

"Of course I didn't fucking kill him." Corbin's eyes flashed. "I'm a thief, not a murderer. I'd never kill anybody."

"But you're still NW2. I'm sure you know Scotland Yard found the poem and the watch in your bag." Luke still couldn't believe it. "I've been hunting you down the entire time you've been in my bed. Months, Corbin. *Months.*"

"What was I supposed to do? Just announce to you that I was the one you were after? That would've gone over well." Corbin's face was so frustrated that Luke nearly forgot what had happened for a moment. For a split second, it was just him and Corbin again, and he had to check himself from reaching out to touch him. And it hurt all over again when he remembered.

"I *trusted* you," Luke said again.

Corbin didn't answer that. He just looked at Luke for long moments. "You can still trust me, you know."

Luke wanted to laugh. He would've if there'd been anything remotely funny about the past twenty-four hours. "How exactly do you figure that?"

"I love you. I did before, and I still do. None of that was a lie. Nothing was except my job. That's the only thing I lied to you about."

"How the hell am I supposed to know that? How am I supposed to know you weren't using me somehow?"

"For what?"

"I don't know. Information."

"Luke, you didn't have any information—nothing I would've needed anyway. I had no idea who you were for weeks. Not a clue. That night you told me what your real job was, that's when I figured it out. I should've walked away. I know that. I should have never looked back. But I wanted you too much. I was falling for you too damn hard to let it go."

"I don't believe you."

"Fuck!" Corbin yelled. He looked like Luke felt, like he wanted to break things, but he wasn't the one who'd been lied to. Luke had been honest with him from the start. Well, nearly the start. "It was supposed to be one more job, you know? Then I was going to quit for good and just be with you. You'd have never found out. I would have never stolen anything else, and we could've been so damn happy. One more job."

"Why'd you do it?" Luke asked. "If you didn't want to ruin us, why'd you do it?"

Corbin shrugged. He looked more frustrated than Luke had ever seen him. "I'm a fucking idiot."

"That's not a reason. I mean it is, but it's not good enough."

"I don't know. I guess I couldn't not finish what I'd started. It was planned, and it was hanging there, you know? Bothering me. I needed to finish it so I could let it go and be happy with you. Fuck of a lot of good it did me."

"I can't believe you. I can't believe you're sitting here telling me you'd quit being the thief I was hunting so we could *date*." Luke couldn't believe he'd listened to it for a few, brief, insane moments. "Like, do you have any idea how absurd that sounds? I'm a government agent. I'm police. You're a criminal. That's... impossible." Luke jumped out of his chair and paced the room. "You lied to me. I thought we were in love!" he roared.

He wanted to scream and break more things and cry. Luke fucking wanted to cry. He wasn't ready to lose it, wasn't ready to lose everything they'd been building, but it was already gone, locked in a storage cell and bound for who the fuck knows where. It wasn't just the thief they'd caught, it was Luke's illusions of a normal life. He didn't get to have that. He got to have his job. And a bunch of broken shit.

"I'd like to talk to Waterman, please." Corbin said quietly. "I think I might have something that's useful to him."

"Wait, what?" He wasn't nearly done with Corbin. Not even close. "*No*. You don't get to make requests."

Luke shook his head and groaned at the fact that Corbin only knew Waterman's name because of him. He'd used Waterman's name when he'd confessed how close they were to finding NW2, or how much his boss had driven him insane. He'd blabbed about work, and it was his fault that Corbin knew anything about them. Luke was such an idiot. "You don't get to see Waterman."

"Please set the meeting up. I believe I can be of help to him and Scotland Yard with the Hughes case." Corbin's face was placid but studied, like he had to work at holding something in.

"The murder investigation has nothing to do with us."

"Yes, but if I have vital information and you hold it back from them, I don't think they're going to like that very much."

Fuck.

Luke growled. He knew he didn't have a choice. He had to do his damn job as much as he wanted to throw Corbin against the wall and punish him and make him hurt like Luke was hurting and kiss him and kiss him and *kiss* him until everything went away. Until he couldn't remember the sight of Corbin cuffed to that table in the middle of the blood and vomit and death. Everything had changed in that one moment.

"Please go get your boss," Corbin repeated. He didn't look like Corbin anymore, not like the Corbin who'd been trying to convince Luke of his love only moments before. He looked steady, cold, calculating.

Luke couldn't refuse his detainee the right to assist in an ongoing case even if he knew exactly what Corbin was doing. He went for professionalism. "I'll send Waterman in when he has some time on his schedule. Do you need anything to drink?"

"No, I'm fine."

"Ring for someone if you need to use the facilities. You won't get to go alone." Luke didn't know why he found himself talking. He needed to get the hell out of there before he said something stupid. Confessed something stupid.

"I know, Luke. They told me everything already." Corbin's face shifted for a moment, the cold mask broke, and he came through soft and sad. Luke couldn't handle it.

"Of course they did. I'm going to go now."

"Luke...." It was back, and not just for a moment. The pleading, loving face he'd gotten to know so well. "Please stay."

"No, Corbin. I'm going now. Waterman will be in here soon."

IT WAS nearly three hours later when Luke got called into Waterman's office. He was surprised to see Clarke there. No, shocked. It wasn't the first time the director of Scotland Yard had been in their offices, but it had been a while. It usually wasn't very pleasant.

"Afternoon." Luke reached out and shook his hand. He didn't want to, didn't want to play polite. It had been over twenty-four hours since he'd slept. He was exhausted, dirty, and fucking heartbroken, but he still had to be polite. Had to do his damn job whether he wanted to or not.

"Eldridge," Clarke said.

"Luke. Sit." Waterman gestured at the chair across from his desk. Luke sank into it and Clarke sat in the one next to it. He was still too angry to be tired, too worried about what was going to happen to Corbin, and angry that he was worried about Corbin, to even think about falling asleep, but Waterman's chairs were plush and comfortable. He had to admit it felt nice to sit.

"We have come to a bit of a deal here," Waterman said.

"A deal?" Luke asked. He tipped his head to the side.

"Yes. Mr. Ford has proved he can be quite valuable to Scotland Yard in our investigation into Hughes's death. We're going to work with him in return for our recommendation that his sentence be shortened."

"How can he possibly help? He's a thief."

"He's a thief who has been observing our victim and his habits for months. He's had access to accounts, tapped his phones, read his e-mails. It would take us weeks to get the information he can give us in minutes. And he's made contacts all over the city that we'd like to utilize."

"Okay." Luke's heart constricted for a moment at the thought of Corbin having a jail sentence, but then he remembered the months of lying, and he wasn't so sad anymore. An interview didn't sound very bad. Some contacts. "What does that have to do with me?"

"Mr. Ford had a few requests to, um, aid in his cooperation."

Luke all of a sudden didn't have the best feeling about what was about to come. "What do you mean?"

"He'd like to work with you."

Of course he would. "Me." Luke was dumbfounded as to how that was supposed to happen. "I don't work for Scotland Yard. I'm not involved in the case at all."

"I've agreed to let the police contract you as a consultant," Waterman said. "Scotland Yard wants you on this case. Hughes was active on the global scene, both socially and in business. It's a smart precaution."

Right. If you asked Luke, it sounded like a lot of bullshit. Scotland Yard wanted whatever Corbin was dangling in front of their noses, and he was going to use that to get whatever he wanted—including Luke's cooperation.

"You want me to work this case now?" It just got better and better. Corbin, sweet, innocent, "I never lied to you" Corbin was manipulating everyone to suit his purposes, whatever they were, and all Luke could do was sit here and take it up the ass. He wondered if there was anything left in his office to break.

"Yes. Mr. Ford has valuable information about the life and habits of Lord Hughes, and he's happy to get further information from some of his contacts around the city, but he requested that you be his handler instead of the officer I suggested. We're happy to cooperate with him if it helps bring the killer to justice."

"You can't be serious. Nobody does this. You can't *do* this."

"Government agencies cooperate with each other quite regularly, despite your usual procedure," Clarke grumbled.

"I'm not a homicide detective, and Corbin, Mr. Ford, isn't a detective at all. He's a *criminal*. This is totally out of order."

"We're perfectly willing to go along with it in the name of interagency cooperation," Waterman said. Luke wanted to scream, but he was aware it wouldn't be looked on well if he did. It was best to nod and grit his teeth until they fell out of his head. "Scotland Yard wants you on this case."

"Why do I get the feeling there will be more stipulations?"

"He'll need to be equipped with a tracker."

I got the feeling because there are more. Of course.

"Like house arrest." That sounded logical. Clarke and Waterman looked wary, so Luke figured that wasn't the rest of it. He couldn't wait.

"Yes. House arrest but not with proximity to his home. We need him to be mobile so he can get to any area of the city necessary."

Luke knew before they said it. "He's going to be tracked to me instead of his apartment, isn't he? Jesus." He was about to be handcuffed to Corbin until his part of the investigation was over, which couldn't come soon enough.

"We can provide a security detail to accompany you if you feel that Mr. Ford is a danger to your person," Clarke offered.

"Thanks. He's not dangerous, but you are fools if you think he's going to stay put. He's brilliant at escaping from places. If he helps, he should help from here. There's no need to release him."

"We'll be monitoring him very closely. He'll stay put. Besides, he was adamant in his ability to help us. I think Ford is quite motivated to do the right thing in this case."

Waterman gave Luke a long look, like he knew exactly why Corbin requested him and why he wanted to be strapped to Luke's side the entire time. Luke was about ready to punch something. Or someone. Corbin would be a great option.

"Why don't we go get Mr. Ford ready? He'll have to get his monitor attached, and we'll need to work with you so you're aware of how everything operates." Clarke tied things up with his usual efficient pompousness.

"Great. Fantastic."

"And then I'm going to ask you and Ford to go home and get some rest. You've both been up for far too long. You're of no use to us like this."

"I can't believe this is happening."

Clarke stood and nodded. "You'll be doing the city of London a huge favor if Ford can provide us any useful information."

"How long am I stuck with him?" Luke asked.

"Until he's no longer useful. Get whatever he knows out of him, use his contacts, and then we'll bring him in here again and figure out what to do with him with the added bit of Scotland Yard's recommendation."

"Fine."

It wasn't fine. It was awful and a huge mess, and Luke could still remember how Corbin tasted early in the morning when they'd just woken up and he had miles of warm skin wrapped around him and *no*. He was a felon. A criminal. Luke's responsibility, not his boyfriend. He'd never been so angry in his life. He knew what Corbin was doing, and it wasn't going to fucking work.

"I'll be at my desk. Please let me know when you're ready to release Ford," he said.

LUKE DIDN'T do anything in his office. Mainly he sat there and stared at the wall. In less than an hour, Corbin would be his again, something that earlier that day would've seemed impossible. But the thing was... he didn't know if he wanted him. Yeah, he wanted him. Hell yeah. But even though Luke couldn't forget Corbin's skin or his taste or the way he laughed when Luke said something dumb, he couldn't forget the lie either. Couldn't forget that same guy who looked right at him and told him he was in love had lied to him. Wasn't even close to the person Luke thought he was.

Luke didn't know if he wanted to kill Corbin, tear him limb from limb, or throw him in bed and tear all his clothes off until they were naked and sweaty and *right* again. He supposed he'd see when the opportunity arose. Which, judging by the fact that they were leading Corbin out of the holding area and into the main offices, was a lot sooner than he'd imagined.

IT'S SHOW time.

CHAPTER NINE

ONE OF the agency cars hired pulled up in front to take Luke and Corbin back to his place. Corbin didn't know what to do. On one hand, he was free. To a point. With a decent amount of effort, he could probably escape if he really wanted to. But he wanted Luke more, as insane as it sounded. He wanted the chance to win Luke back and show him he wasn't completely untrustworthy, and somehow that was more important to him than his freedom. Corbin had realized he was fucked months ago. It wasn't exactly a big shock this time around.

He slid into the back of yet another big dark car, this time with Luke next to him, and he cringed when the door slammed shut. Too many doors had been slammed shut on him lately. It wasn't his favorite sensation.

If Corbin had expected Luke, *his* Luke, in the car with him, he'd have been very unhappy with the results, because he sure as hell didn't get Luke. He got taciturn, unpleasant Agent Eldridge, who kept to his side of the car and shot Corbin distrustful looks every few seconds.

"I'm not going to bolt, you know. I want to help fix this." Corbin figured saying that couldn't hurt.

"Yeah, thanks for getting me involved in a case that has dick to do with me or my department, by the way." Luke stared at him. "Nice way to manipulate the situation to your benefit."

"I want to help," Corbin repeated. And sure, he'd manipulated things to his benefit. What was he going to do? Put his tail between his legs and let Interpol send him to the highest bidder without doing a damn thing to make his situation better? That went against everything he'd ever trained himself to be.

"I don't trust you," he finally said. "I don't know what you're going to do, obviously. Everything I thought I knew was a huge fucking lie."

This isn't going to go well.

"I just told you. I'm not lying. I didn't kill Hughes, but I feel like I'm in the middle, and I want to fix it."

"Absolutely. Of course. Public Servant Corbin Ford wants to do the right thing." He couldn't have rolled his eyes harder if they fell out of his head and did an Irish jig around the car.

"And I want them to get rid of my sentence too. I am in it a little bit for myself."

"You think they're going to drop your sentence? Corbin, you've stolen millions of dollars' worth of goods. Hundreds of millions. You're out of your mind if you think any of this is really going to help you."

"I know I have. I can give some of it back, you know. Most of it actually. I don't spend all that much money."

"Would you?"

He shrugged. He didn't know what he'd be willing to do to get Luke back. Probably just about anything, which he hadn't actually known about himself until he realized Luke was slipping from his grasp. "Let's just solve this case and see what happens."

Luke gave him another look. "We're not going to solve the case. We're going to provide information and contacts to Scotland Yard so their *detectives* can solve the case. I might be working with them on this, but I'm not going to bend over backwards to make you look good. That's how this works. It's not going to be Luke and Corbin playing Sherlock Holmes."

Corbin tried to make a joke. "You caught me in the act. I told you I've always wanted to be Watson."

Luke didn't respond other than to turn and stare out the window.

Tough crowd.

Apparently it was going to take a lot more than a joke or two to break Luke out of that pissed-off agent shell. If he could do it at all. Corbin had to believe he could.

"So—"

Luke cut him off. "I'm tired. I've been up all night. I really can't get into the case yet, and I honestly don't know if I can talk to you."

"You just were."

"I forgot for a split second, but I'm remembering again now. Please be quiet."

CORBIN SAT against the cool black leather seat and watched as London flowed by. It was late afternoon, he imagined, judging by the time he'd spent sitting in dark holding rooms and talking to Clarke. Luke had to be starving and tired. Corbin was both of those things. He thought of where they were going, Luke's bright, light-filled flat, his plush bed, the soft couch. It was hard not to imagine things as they had been only days before. Less than that. Corbin could be fairly sure it wasn't going to be like that this time.

They took the route through Soho and pulled onto Camden's high street. It was crowded as usual: tourists, locals, sidewalks teeming with life and color, leather jackets and crazy spiked hair. It felt different already now that he was with Luke but not *with* him. Less welcoming. Corbin tugged at his pant leg and made sure his anklet was covered. He didn't like it. He didn't like the leash.

"We're here," Luke announced quietly when they pulled up to his building, like Corbin hadn't been there a million times. He supposed it was for the benefit of the agent driving them. He didn't know what other reason there'd be. "Don't leave my side."

"Remember, they're monitoring me. Scotland Yard wouldn't *let* me leave your side."

"I remember. Pretty hard to forget isn't it?"

"Besides, I wouldn't even if I could. I don't want to, Luke. I want to do this."

"Right. I believe you've said that."

The police had a car with two officers following them discreetly, plus the two in their car. He supposed they'd park outside Luke's building that night and make sure Corbin didn't pull anything. He wished he could tell them not to waste their manpower. He wasn't planning on doing anything but sticking right by Luke's side.

He got out of the car and followed Luke to the front of the building. He'd gotten a key to Luke's place a few weeks before. The first time for that in his whole life. He'd loved that key and put it on his key ring right away, couldn't stop grinning for hours. Luke probably wanted it back. Corbin decided not to mention it. It was hard not to touch Luke like they always had before, but he kept a respectful distance as he followed him up the two stories of stairs to his flat.

"You can take the first shower," Luke muttered. "I obviously don't have to tell you where anything is." He looked like he was sorry that Corbin had ever been in his place before so Corbin didn't dare suggest they share. Luke was still shooting glares at him, so the thought of them together in the shower was more like a nice dream than any sort of reality. He washed quickly, perfunctorily. It was awkward to dry off with the tracking anklet in place, a reminder of who he was now. Property of Interpol until he'd served his purpose and then who knows what they'd honor. Still, it was worth it, as insane as that sounded.

He pulled his drawer open and grabbed some sweats and a shirt. It would probably piss Luke off that he still had his drawer of clothes, but Corbin wasn't going to sleep in what he'd had on for nearly twenty-four hours, no matter how mad the reminder made Luke.

He found Luke sitting on the couch. "Your turn. I'll make you some dinner."

"I ordered pizza," Luke said shortly. "Don't even think of pulling any shit when I'm in the shower." Luke hauled himself up off the couch and turned toward the bathroom.

"I wasn't going to," Corbin said quietly. He sat on the couch and laid his head back on the cushions. He waved Luke toward the shower. "I told you, you can trust me. I'm not going to bolt. Just go shower. You look like hell."

"Fuck you," Luke mumbled. He definitely wasn't joking.

CORBIN FELL halfway asleep waiting for Luke to get out of the shower. Even with everything that had happened, even with the mess he'd made, Luke's apartment was still the most comfortable place he'd ever been. The only place he'd ever really felt like he was at home. Of course, he'd ruined that, hadn't he?

Luke gave him another dark look when he came out from the shower. He looked fucking gorgeous in a pair of basketball shorts and a tank top. Corbin wanted him still. More than ever since he was so out of reach. They sat silently waiting for dinner, then ate their pizza silently as well, not even bothering to turn the television on.

Finally Luke spoke. "I'm going to go to take a nap. I'll grab you a pillow and blanket."

"Luke." The question must've been in his eyes.

Luke made an incredulous face. "No. Absolutely not. Have you lost your mind?"

"I won't be able to sleep out here."

"Then you take the bed. I'll sleep on the couch." Luke grumbled. He went to the closet and got out the pillow and blanket. "Are you going?"

"What do you want, Luke?"

"I want to take a nap. And I want you to leave me the hell alone until we have to work. Get it in your head that nothing about us is the way it was two days ago. Then we might be able to deal with things."

IT WAS dark by the time Corbin woke up. He had that weird, heavy feeling he always got when he fell asleep in the middle of the day. It was disorienting to say the least. It took him a while to remember where he was, what had happened, and why everything was definitely not right. He was alone in Luke's bed, and he heard the television humming quietly from the living room. Part of him wanted to cower in Luke's room until morning, but he had to face him if he was ever going to think about getting Luke to forgive him. *That's never gonna happen. He looks at you and sees a criminal.*

Corbin had already seen bits and pieces come through, a moment here, a second there, when Luke looked at him and saw the guy he'd fallen in love with. Didn't mean that guy was going to come back permanently. Corbin didn't know why he had to do this, why he had to convince Luke he was for real and he really loved him. They probably didn't have a chance in hell of ever working again, even if they'd had one at the beginning, but he still had to do it.

He dragged himself out of Luke's pillowy bed and made his way to the living room. Luke had more pizza on his plate, cold from sitting for hours in the fridge, and he was watching what looked like soccer.

Corbin went to the kitchen and got another slice of pizza for himself before he settled on the couch. He wanted to sit next to Luke like he always had, so their sides squished up against one another and Luke eventually slung an arm across Corbin's shoulders. That obviously wasn't a good idea. Instead, he stayed politely in his corner and watched TV with Luke for a few hours. Silently.

"My sleep schedule's all fucked." Luke finally said. "I think I'm going to try to fall asleep. We've got a long day in front of us tomorrow." His voice was curt, professional. A little pissed still. It wasn't what Corbin would call happy Luke—not even a little bit—but it was better.

"I'll sleep out here so you don't hurt your back," Corbin said.

Luke looked at him. Corbin thought he was going to say thank you but instead he sneered. "I can't fucking believe you dragged me into this. Why?"

"I'm sorry. I just couldn't think of another way."

"Another way to what? Remind me every day that my boyfriend is a criminal?"

"Boyfriend?"

"Ex," Luke growled.

"I deserved that. It was stupid to even ask. I wanted to make this up to you. I don't care about Scotland Yard, but if I proved—" Corbin cut himself off. "Never mind. You're not really interested, are you? You're just angry."

"Fucking right I'm angry. First you make a fool out of me with the lying, and now you're going to parade me in front of people you know I don't particularly like, who like me even less, and make me do a job I'm barely trained to do. How exactly do you think I'm going to help you?"

At least he had Luke talking. Talking was always better than silence. Corbin couldn't work with silence, couldn't remind Luke of what they used to be. He could remind Luke of what they were to each other as long as they had things to say.

"You're *smart*. Smarter than any of the people Clarke has working for him. I can find information about Hughes, a lot more than the official people have access to. You wouldn't believe what my family is capable of, and I'm one of them. I can get you places you can't get with Scotland Yard or with Interpol. But *you* can talk to people and help me figure out what it means."

"I really wish I hadn't heard that," Luke said. He raked a hand through his hair.

"It won't be illegal. Really." It sounded like it was, and Corbin wished so much that he hadn't just said that. It didn't help anything.

"Jesus, Corbin. Is there an end to the trouble you've caused me?"

"Do you want to just turn me in? Tell them the deal is off? You can. I deserve it." Corbin obviously didn't want that. But he thought that maybe Luke still had enough feelings buried under his anger that he wouldn't do that.

Luke made a pissy noise and pushed himself off the couch. "I'm going to bed. Be ready to get this shit taken care of. I don't want to drag it out."

"Luke, you really are good at this. You figured out where I'd be last night, didn't you? The police didn't call you, did they? You already knew."

"Yes, we knew. But it wasn't all me. I'm part of a team. I don't know what you expect me to do here on my own."

"Just do your job. I'll do my best to help."

Luke didn't say anything else. He turned and walked into his bedroom and shut the door.

LUKE WAS about to pass out when his phone buzzed. He stared at the caller ID for a long time before he connected.

"Hey, Trish," he said softly. As much as he didn't want to fucking talk to anyone, he did kind of want to hear her voice. He'd had the day from hell. No, whatever was worse than hell. It was nice to have a friend to talk to.

"Hey, babe. I know you're not okay, so I won't even bother asking. This whole thing is crazy."

"What did Rob tell you?"

"That Corbin is NW2. That they thought he'd killed someone before he was cleared." Her voice shook.

Luke had to remind himself to be gentle. As hurt as he was, as *angry* as he was, he had to remember Trish loved Corbin too, and she didn't have Luke and Rob's job to fall back on. This whole thing had to be hitting her hard. He had no idea what they'd tell the girls when Corbin disappeared. They'd fallen for him as much as everyone else.

"That's all you know?"

"Is there more *to* know?"

Luke flopped back onto his bed. "I probably shouldn't get into this with you. I don't know the protocol on this case."

"Luke. I'm worried. Tell me what's happening so I know you're okay." She made a noise. "Sort of okay, at least. I can't imagine what you're feeling right now."

Luke couldn't get into what he was feeling. If he did, he might start throwing things again. Feeling was bad. He had to get the job done and try not to get too angry. "I'm working with Corbin. He made a deal with Scotland Yard and Waterman to help with the case in return for their recommendation that his sentence be lowered."

Trish was silent for a long time. "You've got to be fucking with me."

"No, unfortunately I'm not. He's here right now"

"Can he even do that?"

"He did. I was too tired to get into it today, but I guess whatever he told them he could do was convincing enough for them to put aside their grudges and corral me into consulting with Scotland Yard."

"Consulting?"

"Babysitting Corbin? Consultant is my official title until this shit-show is over. Hopefully I'll give them enough the first day or two to get this whole thing done with so I can never ever see him again."

"Babe. Do you really mean that?" Trish sounded like she was on the verge of tears.

No, please don't cry. If she started, Luke honestly didn't know what he'd do. He was tired and still so, so hurt. He gritted his teeth, then sighed. "I don't know. I don't know what I mean. You know I told him I loved him a couple days ago?"

"Shit," Trish whispered.

"Yeah. The fucked up thing is I think I still do." He didn't know how he could push those feelings out of him, clench his jaw and concentrate until they seeped out of his pores and disappeared. But as much as he wanted to kill Corbin for what he'd done, there was another smaller part of him that wanted nothing more than to pull him close and tell him everything was going to be okay.

"Of course you do. He loves you too, you know. Whatever he was lying to you about, it wasn't that."

"I don't think it's enough. He fucked with me so much. He made me think we had a future. He made me think we were something real."

"You *were* real. I know what love looks like, and it was all over Corbin's face every time he looked at you."

"He's out in my living room with a tracking anklet on." Luke couldn't let himself forget reality, as much as he wanted to.

"Oh, sweetie."

"Listen, T. I'm not really in the mood to dwell on it. It sucks, and I have to move on and do my job until he's out of my life. End of story."

"Luke, that can't be the end of the story. You two were so perfect."

"He's a *felon*."

"But you love him. I know this is going to sound crazy to someone like you, but sometimes that's what matters most. Not the rest of it."

"I've gotta go," Luke said. He hung up before Trish had the chance to answer. He couldn't do it. Couldn't get into it with her and hear her sympathy and her ultimate belief in love. He couldn't let her tell him all the reasons why he should let Corbin stay in his life. It couldn't work. To even consider it was impossible.

Luke flopped down on his bed and squeezed his eyes shut. Didn't work. When he opened them, everything was exactly the same as it had been.

IF CORBIN hoped it would be different in the morning, well, he should've known better. He'd sat up half the night on the couch, knowing Luke was right there on the other side of the bedroom door and he couldn't fucking have him. He'd heard him talking on the phone, although not the individual words, and known Luke was talking about him. He'd sounded so angry and sad and pissed off at the world. Corbin knew it was his fault. Hell, *obviously* it was his fault. All he wanted to do was fix it. Fix him and Luke. Obvious, again, that it was impossible. Even in the face of all the relentless obviousness, he'd still try.

He'd fallen asleep somewhere before dawn when the sun rose through shades neither one of them had remembered to screw shut the night before. He knew he only had about an hour before they had to get up and get to crime fighting, but every time he closed his eyes, all he saw was Luke's destroyed face back at Hughes's mansion. It had killed him. He knew what a risk Luke had taken giving away his heart, because Corbin had taken that same risk, and it hurt just as bad for him even if he'd been the one at fault.

When he heard Luke go to his shower, he'd probably been asleep for an hour, if that. But Corbin's eyes popped open like a dog waiting for his master to come home, and he couldn't close them again. He pictured Luke in there, naked and warm and soapy. He probably wouldn't get to see that again other than in his memories, which sucked. It sucked a fucking lot.

He sat up and scrubbed the lack of sleep out of his eyes. He wasn't ready to be on the other side of the law. Didn't even know if he could find anything to significantly lower his sentence. But that wasn't the point. The point was to prove to Luke he was sorry. That much, he'd make sure he did. Luke came out of the shower silently and slipped into his room, presumably to get dressed. Corbin needed some of his clothes, but there was no way in hell he'd burst into Luke's room, no matter how much he wanted to watch him slip on trousers and a shirt, and run his hands through his damp hair. Corbin hadn't appreciated the right to do that when he'd had it. Not enough, at least.

He waited until Luke was dressed and out in the hallway before he stood. "Do you mind if I grab some clothes?" he asked. It was scary to even talk to Luke.

Luke sighed. "No. It's fine. Leave the door open."

"Luke, I'm not going to steal from you. Jesus."

"There's a balcony in that room. I don't know exactly how good you are at scaling buildings, but I imagine you can probably do this building in your sleep."

"Yeah, with half of Scotland Yard below us, in broad daylight on a crowded street. I'm not going to escape. I want to do this. I want to stay here. When will you believe that?"

"Never, probably. I don't believe anything you say."

Ouch. And totally deserved.

Corbin didn't want to push it, so he went into Luke's room. His stuff, the stuff that used to be all over the place in drawers and on hangers, was neatly folded on top of Luke's dresser. The message was clear. He didn't belong there anymore. Corbin wanted to cry. Like actually cry, which he hadn't done since he was about thirteen.

He picked up the piles of his belongings and brought them out to the living room. There was room on top of the television console. He put his clothing there and tucked the shoes off to the side.

He couldn't look at Luke while he set his stuff down in neat piles. If he did he might break down, and he didn't want Luke to think he was looking for sympathy. After he organized everything, he grabbed a few things and went into the bathroom to quickly deal with washing. It wasn't much fun alone. He didn't like it. So he showered quickly and dressed, and met Luke in the dining room, where he was drinking coffee and looking at his phone.

"There's food. You know where it is. Feel free to have coffee."

Luke wouldn't have had to say anything before. Corbin knew where the food was. He'd bought half of it. It was weird being treated like a very unwelcome guest in the place that had nearly been his home. He went to the fridge and took some of his own organic granola and the coconut milk he'd purchased himself and made a bowl of cereal. "I'll buy some more later today. You're low on eggs," Corbin said.

"You're not going to the store without me."

"Okay. Then we'll go together after work. You need eggs."

Luke made a face. "Isn't this domestic. Work and breakfast and shopping together. We're the happy little family, aren't we?"

"Please don't be mean. I told you I loved you, and I do. *So* much. I know I lied about who I was, but you don't have to be mean. I didn't want to hurt you."

"Screw you." Luke glanced at his phone again. "Hurry up. We have a lot of work to do today."

THEY WERE quiet in the car on the way to the office, escorted by Scotland Yard again—officers in the car, officers behind them in another car. It was stifling. Corbin had to remind himself he'd signed up for this. The alternative was far worse. "I want to work in my own building," Luke said. "We might be consulting for the police, but I know my workspace better."

"That's fine," Corbin said. Like he cared where they worked as long as he got to be near him. It was weird, how it hurt so bad but he couldn't even think of giving it up. Even angry Luke was better than no Luke at all.

Luke directed the policemen to drive them to Interpol's office and told them to feel free to come in if they wanted to. He was efficient and polite with the police, who'd done nothing to harm him. Corbin loved watching him operate. It was so unfair that he finally got to see Luke in his element in such a bad situation.

When they got to the office, it was busy and loud and full of people doing important crime-solving things, Corbin imagined. They all turned to stare at him and Luke when they walked through the door.

"Jesus, people," Luke finally said. "I'm the same person I was yesterday, and Ford isn't going to bite. I'll be at my desk with him if you need anything."

Ford. A new level of feeling like shit. Still, he held his head high and followed Luke to his office. Corbin sighed a long sigh of relief when they were alone with the door closed. It was better than having half of Interpol London staring at him like he was a parasite.

Well. That was a promising start.

FOR THE next few minutes, they did a lot more of that silent staring shit that seemed to be Luke's new MO when it came to him. It was frustrating as hell, and Corbin wanted no more of it. If nothing else, they had a job to do, and that job was finding Scotland Yard some suspects. Or at least some info on Hughes they didn't already have.

"Luke, we can't just sit here silently all day."

"Call me Eldridge," Luke snapped.

Ouch. Again. "You can't be serious. I'm not going to call you that after you've been *inside* me."

"Something I'd rather not be reminded of at the moment, thanks."

Corbin wondered how many times he could set himself up for pain before he got the picture and stopped. Infinity, he imagined. "Luke. Let's just do this."

"Fine. We'll work. So, first things first," Luke said. "Tell me whatever the fuck you told Clarke that made him want to give you a chance."

Luke whipped out a notebook and pen and stared at Corbin again. Enough with the fucking stare.

"I know his schedule said he'd be out of town that night, and he sure as hell wasn't."

"That doesn't mean anything. Plans change. There's no way that's enough for Interpol and fucking Scotland Yard to have given you a chance."

Corbin gave him a look. "There were other things, obviously, but the schedule matters. Schedules don't change at the drop of a hat. Not for people like him." Corbin shook his head. "He had vast holdings and businesses, and he was a diplomat. His week was usually triple-checked by his staff, his wife, his secretary. He's one of those people who's never in the wrong place. I know that too. Something seriously fucked up was going on for him to not have been where he was supposed to be."

"So you're saying he slipped out of his schedule for some reason, and we should start there?"

"It's as good a place as any."

"Fine. What else? That can't be all you gave them."

"It wasn't any one piece of information." Corbin shrugged. "It was more like the fact that I already knew things they hadn't learned yet, and it was obvious I can learn more and quickly, like I told you last night. Like, he was married, but from what I can tell, it wasn't for a whole lot more than show. He and his wife didn't tend to be in the same place at the same time."

"I don't think that's exactly news in the upper crust."

"No. And obviously he was totally loaded. I always want to know if there's debt hiding behind the tapestries and china cabinets. Not even close with this guy. There are landslides of money piled up."

"Are we looking at the wife?" Luke asked. It was the first time he looked genuinely curious rather than bored.

"I say we look at everyone. Spouses are usually the first place to look, aren't they?"

"I don't know. I'm not a homicide detective."

"What? You've never watched TV?" Corbin rolled his eyes. "I know you're like being a dick for entertainment, but can you stop? I get the picture. You hate me. You don't want to be here. So let's just do the job. Like I said."

"You don't get to talk to me like that," Luke said quietly. "You ruined my trust, which I don't give out lightly, and you broke my fucking heart." He looked down at his desk for a minute. His hand was clenched around the pen. "You're a *criminal*."

"Thanks for reminding me," Corbin said. His chest was tight, and it was getting hard to breathe. "I'd almost forgotten."

CHAPTER TEN

CORBIN DIDN'T like being in the Interpol offices. It would've been different before, watching Luke be all powerful and sexy and in charge, with Corbin by his side by choice instead of effectively handcuffed to him because of Corbin's manipulation. Nobody seemed very interested in talking to him. They sure as *hell* were interested in talking to Luke, though. Waterman's assistant, Rosie, who, if Corbin remembered correctly, was also his daughter and one of Luke's "best friends," giggled at Luke like some little schoolgirl, fluttering her big dumb lashes. Then there was the efficient-looking blonde agent who followed him around and another desk clerk who tracked Luke's movements with her eyes. Corbin wondered if Luke was even aware of it. He did a good job of ignoring it.

"Are we going to go to Hughes's house? Talk to his staff?" Corbin asked. Luke had been in the middle of talking to giggly-flirt assistant number one. Rosie. Right. Rosie had leaned closer to Luke and was in the middle of adjusting her tight-ass sweater. He didn't want to talk to Hughes's staff as much as he wanted to get the hell out of the Interpol office.

"Yeah. In a little bit. I have my own job to do first." Luke turned away from Corbin as soon as he was done speaking, effectively dismissing him.

Corbin didn't like it. Not at all. Luke was hurt. He got it. But they were in this thing now, and verbally stabbing Corbin like he had over and over was somehow worse than what he'd done. Sure, he'd stolen some things. A lot of things, okay. But he'd repeatedly told Luke he loved him, and everything they had was so very real to him. What about that did Luke not get?

I'm being stupid. Of course he's going to punish me until the end of time. Why did I even hope for something different? Fine. Two can play that game. And if you think you're better at them than I am, Luke Eldridge? Pshh. Right.

"Why don't I go set the meeting up, then? I'm sure you won't mind me using the phone in your office." Corbin smiled serenely like nothing at all was wrong and went into Luke's office, shutting the door behind him. He guessed he had about a minute before Luke managed to get out of the conversation he was currently in and come barging in like he was saving the day from Corbin doing something reckless. He decided to use the time wisely and dialed the number they had on hand for Hughes's assistant. Wouldn't want Luke to think he was bluffing just to get Velcro Rosie off his ass.

"Hi, this is Corbin Ford. I'm working with Interpol and Scotland Yard, investigating Lord Hughes's murder. I'd like to stop by today—"

The door slammed open. "Give me the phone," Luke growled.

That was about a minute. Maybe even less.

Corbin smiled internally. "Of course. This is Lord Hughes's assistant, Jeffrey. I was just setting up a time for us to stop by and interview him and the household staff. Coincidentally, I believe Lady Hughes is available on Mondays as well. Must be our lucky day." Corbin had to hold himself in from giving Luke a smartass smirk. At least he had his attention.

"I'll deal with it," Luke grumbled.

"LADY HUGHES. Thank you for agreeing to meet with us," Luke said.

They'd already spoken with Jeffrey and the rest of the household staff. Nobody had anything new to add to what Scotland Yard had already gotten out of them. Officially, that is. Luke had a strong feeling the assistant, Jeffrey, knew something. Probably quite a lot of things. They always did. Assistants were the core of everything that went on in the upper echelons, and they knew every dirty secret there was to know. But the guy wasn't talking, and Luke couldn't exactly give him a reason to do so if he had no proof he was hiding things. If Jeffrey blabbed all over the place about his former employer's habits, he'd have a hard time finding a new job. Those sorts of things always got out. Luke figured they'd have to go another route. Maybe the pissed off wife.

Here goes.

The icy Lady Hughes was probably their best bet. She hadn't spoken to Scotland Yard yet. She'd been detained and then busy and then unable to comment, and their hands had been tied because of her status. Luke thought it was a stroke of luck they'd happened to catch her. She sat behind her library desk like a queen, staring down at the ants below her. Her hair was perfect and a little scary, iron gray and pinned in a neat bun. Her clothes were the understated kind of expensive. Chanel probably. Luke didn't know. Whatever it was smelled expensive and looked uncomfortable. Pretty much exactly like Lady Hughes herself.

She made a face at Luke. "You might as well call me Sylvia. I'm not Lady Hughes any longer. That honor goes to my sister-in-law now."

"Okay, um, Sylvia." He tried to pretend he wasn't desperately intimidated by her. "I'm Luke Eldridge with Interpol, and this is Corbin Ford. He's a consultant for us."

"What does a consultant do?" she asked.

"I'm knowledgeable about certain subjects," Corbin answered. Luke was proud of him. It was about the best thing he could've said.

"Such as?" Lady Hughes asked. "What is your background?"

Oh, hell no. Luke didn't want to get into Corbin's past, sordid or otherwise, with Lady Hughes. She might not tell them anything if she thought they were fucking around with her, and bringing a criminal on an interview might easily fall into that category. Luke opened his mouth to talk but Corbin beat him to it.

"I'm good with research," he simply said.

Research. I'll take research. She seemed to buy it, because she asked no more questions.

"So, Lady Hughes. Sylvia. I'm sure you know why we're here," Luke continued. He wasn't a big fan of her hospitality, and he wanted to get the interview over as quickly as possible.

"To make sure I didn't kill my husband, I'd imagine. The police have already been by. I doubt I have anything to tell you that my staff didn't already tell them."

She looked so bored with the whole situation, it was almost funny. Luke couldn't help the smile that quirked up the side of his mouth for a moment. "I suppose you could put it that way."

Lady Hughes slid an invitation across the desk. "I was at this dinner party. It started at six and didn't end until nearly midnight. From what I've heard about the time of death, that's a solid alibi."

"And you didn't notice your husband's body lying across the bed?" Corbin asked. Ironic, Luke thought, since Corbin hadn't noticed it, either.

She gave him a long, disdainful look. "I haven't slept in the same bedroom as my husband in nearly fifteen years. I mostly certainly did not notice that about him. Or anything else. We're not what you'd call close."

"So you live in the same house and don't interact."

She shrugged elegantly. "You could put it that way, yes."

"May I keep this envelope?" he asked.

"Yes. Although it's not going to help you much. My circles and Thomas's were quite connected, but we rarely spoke with the same people." She shrugged again. Not very forthcoming, that one. "I don't really care to discuss this anymore."

"Sylvia. Your husband was murdered. A husband you seem to have no love or even liking for. Aren't you a little concerned the police might notice that?"

"No. Because if they look into it any further, they'll realize it was *very* advantageous for me to keep Thomas alive."

"Care to explain further?"

She shuddered. "It's practically out of a Jane Austen book. The title was Thomas's, not mine. The properties as well. I actually got a rather modest inheritance. The rest of it, including this house in a few weeks, revert to his brother and his wife."

"So, you really wouldn't want him dead." Luke was flabbergasted. That was some crazy shit.

"No. I most certainly did not. I won't pretend that Thomas and I had a close relationship, but I wouldn't want him dead even if I were the killing type. It's quite inconvenient."

"Is there anything you can tell us that would help?"

She sighed, like they were the most annoying thing in her day. "I suppose you could thoroughly check his laptop. I didn't see him often but when I did, he was on that thing like it was his whole life."

"His laptop?" Luke hadn't been told anything about a laptop. Something that needed to be remedied immediately.

"Yes. I gave it to the other detectives. Your people should have it."

Luke made a note to stop by Scotland Yard and get the laptop that had apparently had Hughes's whole life on it. He gestured for Corbin to follow him out of the Hughes mansion.

"YOU THINK the laptop will tell us anything?" Corbin asked once they were out of the house.

"Maybe. If he had much to tell. I'll call in to Clarke and tell him to make it available to us in the morning."

"You think they'll do that?"

"If there's information on there that you can corroborate or elaborate on, yes. They will. It's why you're here, isn't it?"

Another dig. Corbin felt it like a twinge in his chest. It wasn't a new sensation anymore, but he still didn't like it. Luke pulled out his phone and walked a few steps away to make his phone call, like Corbin couldn't hear him requesting to see the laptop. Super top secret. Corbin rolled his eyes. Clarke's goons got closer to Corbin, like they thought just because Luke stepped away, he was going to bolt. He hadn't done it yet. He was getting a little annoyed by the staring. Yeah, he got why they didn't trust him, but they needed to get a grip.

Luke came back a bit later with an annoyed look on his face.

"Clarke says he'll let us take the laptop, but it's encrypted and they can't get shit off of it. He says it's useless."

"I might be able to," Corbin said quietly.

"You think you can do what a whole team of Scotland Yard-trained computer geniuses can't do?"

"Maybe. I'm good with that kind of stuff." Corbin was more than good with that stuff. And if he wasn't good enough, he knew someone who was. He'd worked with hackers and programmers and guys who could practically build a supercomputer from some toothpicks and a pack of gum. He knew computers like he knew stealing. He wasn't planning to say that in front of Thing One and Thing Two from Scotland Yard, though.

Luke huffed. "Of course you are."

"To be fair, I watched him for a long time. I might have seen him type in passwords a few times. I can take a better guess than people who never saw any of that." He smiled softly at how irritated Luke looked that Corbin could potentially, again, outsmart the police.

"You hungry?" Luke asked abruptly. "I was going to stop for curry on the way home."

"I can cook," Corbin said. He missed their nights in the kitchen already, and it hadn't even been that long since the last one.

"No. None of that shit. No cooking or movies together or anything. We're working on the Hughes case. The end."

"I get the picture. Clearly." Corbin should've known better than to suggest an intimate home-cooked meal. That was beyond the pale for the new Corbin and Luke. Pasta seasoned with ankle tracker didn't work well for Luke's sensibilities. A perverted version of what they'd had. He understood in a way. He'd let Luke have that separation.

"Curry it is."

THEY DROVE in silence to the Indian place, waited in silence, and returned to Luke's apartment in even more, you guessed it, silence. Corbin was about to scream if he didn't get a single word out of Luke. He was literally going to open his mouth and start shouting if that meant he'd get some sort of decent reaction from him.

They ate in the same stultifying silence as before. Corbin heard street noises, the sound of chewing, music coming from the apartment below. He couldn't fucking take it.

"Why won't you even talk to me? I know I got us stuck in this situation, but we're here. Can't you at least talk?"

"You want talk?" Luke asked. He threw his fork into the container of curry. "You wanna hear what I have to say?"

"Yes. Please."

"I *hate* that I still want you," he growled out. "I hate that I look at you, and I can still remember what it felt like to be inside you. I fucking hate that remembering your kisses kept me up all night and that I reach for you so many times every damn minute, and then I remember why I can't touch you. I remember what you did to me, to us."

"I didn't do it to us, Luke. I made the worst mistake of my life going to Hughes's house, but I didn't do it to hurt you."

"What, so you wish you would've not gone there? Just gone to a different job, stolen something else? Kept lying to me?"

"I told you. I wanted to quit when I was done with Hughes. I would've never done it again. I just wanted to be with you."

Luke looked shocked for a moment before he sneered. "Well, that's gone to fucking hell, hasn't it?"

Luke pushed his chair away and stalked out of the room. Corbin followed him. He couldn't let it end here and have another night of chilly weirdness. He needed Luke's touch. He needed that familiar fire all around him. If nothing else, a bit of closure would help.

"Please," he said when he found Luke storming around his room, ripping off his tie and kicking his shoes into the corner.

"Please what, Corbin? Please pretend the past few days didn't happen? Please pretend my entire chest didn't get ripped apart when I saw you handcuffed to that table? You know what my first instinct was? It was to go protect you. To get that horrible thing off your wrist and hold you close. Then I realized what you were doing there. I thought I was going to throw up, right in front of half the police force in London."

"I'm sorry. *So* sorry."

"I know you are. You've said it a million times. What do you want me to do about it?"

"Touch me. Please. I won't ask again, just this one time." He knew it was crazy to ask. Luke was so angry, and they had zero chance of going back to where they were. But he needed it so bad.

"Fuck!" Luke shouted. Then he crossed the room in three huge strides and pushed Corbin against the wall.

He slammed their mouths together in a punishing kiss. Corbin didn't care. He gloried in it, in the contact he had been sorely missing.

"I want you," he breathed into Luke's mouth.

"Take off your clothes," Luke said.

Corbin was more than eager to comply. He pulled off his shoes and slacks and the button-up he'd put on that morning in an attempt to look respectable. He stripped off his socks and briefs and crawled into

Luke's bed once again. It smelled familiar, and the sheets were soft against his skin. Home.

Luke stripped and followed him down until Corbin was crowded against the bed in the very best way. Luke nudged his knee between Corbin's thighs. Corbin opened happily.

"Hold on."

Luke fumbled around for lube and the condoms they'd nearly worked their way through. Corbin almost reached to help him, but he didn't want to say or do anything to make Luke change his mind. To make him not want what they were about to do.

"I wish I didn't remember how good you feel," Luke muttered. Then he sank two gentle fingers in deep. Even in his anger, he was sweet with Corbin, touched him the way he liked to be touched. Corbin arched into it.

"Keep going."

"You drive me fucking insane." His words were paired with one last deep thrust of his fingers before he pulled them out. Corbin helped him with the condom, and before he knew it, Luke was there, right back where he belonged. Corbin squeezed Luke's hips with his thighs and groaned as he felt Luke's cock thick and heavy inside him.

"That's what I needed. Perfect," he murmured. "I missed you. Even in just a couple days, I missed you."

"Don't," Luke said lowly. "Just don't."

It was quiet after that, other than groans and heavy breaths. Corbin didn't speak with his mouth, only his hands, soothing Luke, telling him it was exactly what both of them needed.

"Why do you do this to me?" Luke ground out just before his body shuddered into Corbin's.

"You do it right back," Corbin said. He went to finish himself, but his hand was slapped away. Luke rained biting kisses all over his neck as he stroked Corbin to completion. They collapsed on the bed in silence, only their heaving breaths punctuating the silence of the room.

"D-Do you want me to go to the living room?" he finally asked. Corbin didn't *want* to ask. He only wanted to curl into Luke's arms and fall asleep to the hope that he might have actually gotten through to him. Luke's chest was sweaty against his back. He didn't move.

"It's fine. Just stay here."

"Are you sure?" Corbin asked.

"Go to sleep, Corbin. Just… go to sleep."

WHEN HE woke in the morning, Corbin was still in Luke's bed. They were curled together naked, the heat from the morning sun already splashing across their skin. Corbin felt like he could breathe finally. He could breathe for however long it lasted.

CHAPTER ELEVEN

"LUKE, I have it. I'm in."

Of course Corbin got into the laptop. Didn't even take him that long. After a few phone calls Luke pointedly ignored in case he didn't want to know what was being said, Corbin had spent an hour or two clicking around the computer. And presto.

Luke wasn't pissed about it. They needed the information, but he was annoyed that Corbin was as good as he said he was. And he was trying to get the night before out of his head. Every time he closed his eyes, all he could picture was Corbin, arched and moaning, warm, tight, crying out how much he loved Luke. It was hard to concentrate on anything else. Apparently Corbin didn't have that problem.

He stalked over and slumped down on the couch next to Corbin, who had Hughes's laptop open on the coffee table. He'd indeed gotten it to the main screen, but it didn't look like much. Just an innocuous computer.

"What first?"

"Check his schedule, I suppose." Luke didn't know what to do with the damn thing other than bash it all over the place and curse Lord Hughes for getting shot and getting Corbin caught—and shit. How could Luke already be at the place where he simply wished he didn't know? Where he and Corbin could go back to what they had been before, and he could be ignorant and in love and happy again. He was at that place. Zero doubt.

Corbin thought about it for a moment. "Why don't we look through his e-mails first. We can deal with the schedule when we have the official one in front of us. Unless you want to take a trip to my place for my computer. I downloaded the one his assistant kept, but I can't get to it remotely."

"Of course you did."

"Quit being annoyed that I'm good at my job." Corbin made a face. "Usually at least. I sucked enough at it one night that you managed to catch me."

Luke decided to ignore that. "How are you going to find his e-mail?"

"Let me see if he has any login data stored," Corbin said. He looked around the computer for a few minutes before he shook his head. "Nothing. I suppose we can check all the usual suspects and hope he didn't sign off every time he used it. I don't feel like figuring out another password. That first one was a pain."

An hour and a half was a pain? Luke wondered how Corbin would like it if he had to spend *months* hunting down one elusive pain in *his* ass who had turned out to be right in front of him all along.

Corbin tried a few different e-mail servers. He made a happy little grunting noise when he landed on one.

"He has an account on here. I don't know what it'll find us, but it's still signed in."

"You honestly think he was doing illegal business dealings on Yahoo?" Luke asked with a snort, peering over Corbin's shoulders.

"Of course not. But maybe this will give us some contacts we didn't know he had, like... Letitia Bixley. Have you heard that name? Because I sure as hell haven't. There are an awful lot of e-mails in here from her."

Luke tried to recollect that name in the paperwork, but it wasn't anywhere. According to everything they had on Lord Hughes, Letitia Bixley didn't exist. Corbin casually clicked on one of the e-mails and started reading aloud.

"'Thomas, darling, I miss your kiss'—Oh. *Oh.* I, um, don't think Miss Bixley was a business associate. At least not the kind we were looking for."

"Lord Hughes had a *mistress*?" Luke asked. He raised his brows. It wasn't a shock when he thought about it, but there hadn't been anything about her in the Scotland Yard file. Lord Hughes seemed to have had a hell of a lot of things that weren't visible to the public eye.

"Looks like it. Damn," Corbin said quietly. "How the hell could I have missed this?" He opened a few more e-mails. "Seemed like Miss Bixley wanted Hughes to leave his wife sooner so they could move to the country away from 'all of it.'"

"Hughes was leaving his wife?"

"This just keeps getting better," Corbin said.

"No kidding." Luke wiped his palms on his jeans. "I think you and I need to pay another visit to Lady Hughes, don't you?"

THE ESTEEMED Lady Sylvia Hughes didn't seem much happier to see them the second time than she had the first. She had on another prissy dress, low heels, a sweater draped over her shoulders to ward off the glacial air conditioning in their spacious townhouse, and a dour look on her face.

"I thought I'd handled the two of you already. What more could you possibly want?" She looked at her watch.

Luke figured they had five minutes tops before they were going to be shuffled out of there. "Were you aware that your husband had a mistress?" Luke asked. He figured in these cases, it was best to jump right in rather than play coy. Plus he thought Lady Hughes could handle it. She was a tough one.

"Of course," she said dismissively. "Strumpet from up north." If there was one thing Luke had learned, it was that Londoners turned their noses up at people from "up north."

"Are you aware your husband was planning on leaving you for her?"

Lady Hughes laughed. Carefree, perfectly comfortable, and absolutely mocking the idea. "Is that what she said? Poor desperate thing. No, my husband was most assuredly not leaving me. There were agreements when we married. He would've been very unhappy financially if he broke them. I don't think he liked anyone enough to part with his money. I didn't say anything about his indiscretions, and he didn't say anything about my credit card charges. It was a well-oiled system."

"Do you know what her name was? Your husband's mistress?"

"I believe you are looking for Letitia Bixley. Did you not know that already? Not very good at your jobs, are you?"

"We did. Just needed confirmation. Sorry to have wasted your time, Lady Hughes."

She waved them away. "Since I'm assuming this is the actual last time we'll be seeing each other, I bid you good day, sir. I hope you find what you're looking for."

Your husband's murderer. That's what we're looking for. Luke really didn't like her or most of the people they'd come in contact with so far in the Hughes case. He was ready for it to be over.

"So we bring Letitia Bixley to Scotland Yard?" Corbin asked when they were once again outside the Hughes mansion. He looked relieved not to be in there. Luke was relieved too. Bad vibes in that house. He shuddered.

"No, actually I'd like to bring her in to Interpol to talk to her. According to Scotland Yard, she doesn't exist. I'd like to see what she knows myself, and our building will be the best place to do that without them getting their noses all tangled into it."

"You don't want to hand this to Clarke?"

No. He didn't. Luke knew if they handed Miss Bixley to Clarke, he was probably fulfilling his obligations and could get rid of Corbin—assuming that Corbin didn't come up with a million other reasons that they needed him. Truth was, he didn't want to do that anymore. He didn't want to drop Corbin altogether. And he didn't want to drop Hughes either. He was *curious.* Whatever part of Luke that respected protocol was overpowered by the part of him that couldn't just drop a case once he'd started unraveling it. The old Luke was back. At least that part of him.

"I think you and I can handle it and see if she really knows anything. You in?"

Corbin gave him a tentative smile. "Yeah. I'm very in."

"THANK YOU for coming in, Miss Bixley."

Hughes's mistress, Letitia Bixley, sank into one of the chairs in the interview room at the Westminster Interpol offices. She looked expensive, but not Lady Hughes's brand of expensive. Different. Flashier somehow with way more jewelry, tighter clothes, overstated fragrance, and she was a good twenty years younger. Luke wondered if it was all for show, if she used her slick sophistication to lure men like Hughes into supporting her lifestyle. He supposed if both parties were in agreement about the arrangement, everything was fine. Things tended to go sour when one party expected more than the other was willing to give and found they weren't going to get what they wanted.

Letitia seemed like the kind of woman who was on the angry side of scorned. It was something to think about for sure.

She crossed her legs and tapped a red nail on the table. "I didn't have much choice, did I? With you coming to my flat and all to request a meeting?" Luke reminded himself to thank Kelly for the favor. "I can't hide behind a title and refuse comment like the ice queen."

"WE'VE SPOKEN to Lady Hughes already, actually. She was quite helpful." Luke raised an eyebrow and stared her down. He needed this woman to talk. "We have some questions about your whereabouts the night Thomas Hughes was murdered."

Letitia shrugged. "I didn't have any plans that evening, and Thomas told me he'd be out of town, so I had a quiet night alone."

"Do you have anyone who can corroborate that?"

"I was *alone*," she said again. She looked annoyed that she was required to participate in the investigation. Not much more cooperative than Lady Hughes. Luke wondered why none of the women in Hughes's life seemed to be all that concerned about finding his killer. Or looked like they didn't even care he was dead. Letitia shifted in her chair and adjusted her skirt, looking around the room while she waited. Didn't make eye contact. Interesting.

"Is there any way we can verify that?"

"I don't bloody well know. Can you check my Netflix activity?" She made a bored face. "I was at home. I don't know my neighbors very well. I loved Thomas. I'd never hurt him. He made me happy."

"Is there anything you can do to help us find whoever actually would hurt him? It would be really useful to us and…." Luke paused. There was something about this woman he didn't like. He wanted to lean on her, but technically he couldn't. She couldn't prove she wasn't there, but they had nothing placing her at the scene, either. "Get rid of some suspects on our current list." He made sure that statement was weighted.

"He's been arguing a lot over the phone with an associate of his," she finally offered. She still looked bored, but it was starting to be obvious to Luke that her boredom was put on. Her eyes still shifted around the room, her posture wasn't relaxed. Something about being in their office was making Miss Bixley nervous.

"Do you know this man's name?" Corbin asked. "Lord Hughes's business associate?"

Luke knew he'd be trying to remember the schedule he'd studied while she spoke.

"Archer Pennington. Lord Wellesley. He's known Thomas for years."

Corbin made a face like he hadn't seen that name, which was odd if they'd been friends for years. "Did you hear what they were arguing about?" he asked.

Letitia shook her head. "If Thomas wanted to talk about things he got up to with the other lords, he could do that with his wife. When they spoke, that is. He and I didn't talk about those things."

"What did you talk about?"

"How he wanted a simple life. How he was tired of the games his wife played."

Luke wasn't buying her story. He knew what lying looked like, and while Corbin had shaken his self-confidence, it was starting to come back. "She told us he had no intention of leaving her for you."

She shrugged. "I suppose we'll never know, will we."

Luke nodded. "Corbin, in the hallway for a moment please?" He pulled Corbin out from the room. "I don't trust her."

"Oh, I don't either. She's not grieving nearly enough for someone who's supposedly in love. Also, I think she knows a hell of a lot more than she's saying. And she's nervous. Did you catch the way she's looking everywhere but at you? This lady knows something. I just can't put my finger on it."

"And we can't hold her. We're not the London police, and we don't have anything on her."

"So we let her go and keep an eye on her. See if she tells us anything by her actions?"

"We have to let her go for sure. And we're going to need to talk to this Pennington guy. If he's as open as the rest of them have been, it's not going to be a big help."

"You want to give the name and the computer to Clarke and let him and his officers deal with it?" Corbin asked. Just like with Letitia

Bixley, he seemed inclined to at least give Luke the choice of following protocol.

He didn't want to, just like with Letitia. If he'd been asked that on the first day, he'd have said yes, give them the information and quit while he still had a tiny bit of his heart intact. But he wanted to follow through. The investigator in him wanted to know the truth, and the rest of him wasn't ready to give Corbin up yet.

"No. Let's find this guy ourselves. Clarke wanted me on the case? I'm on it."

CHAPTER TWELVE

ARTHUR PENNINGTON, Lord Wellesley, lived in a crumbling old manor outside York. It had taken them all morning to get there after an early start. Four hours stuck in a car with Luke had been a bit awkward, even if the scenery was lush and gorgeous.

Things were better than they had been, but it wasn't the romantic jaunt to the countryside Corbin had always pictured when it would've involved picnic baskets, kisses, and probably a night in a romantic bed and breakfast. Still, the rolling hills were pretty and green, the hedgerows charming, and every little town they rolled by lovelier than the last. He liked England except for the frigid, rainy winters. Too bad he wasn't going to get to stay.

The door was opened by a staff member, who informed them Lord Wellesley was out in the gardens and he wasn't receiving visitors. That greeting changed quickly when Luke said they were consulting with Scotland Yard and investigating a murder. He was surprised the staff member didn't require more identification than his Interpol badge. Maybe that was enough to scare him into cooperating. Whatever the reason, he led them through the house to a structured rose garden in back.

There were several workers weeding and trimming a very impressive display of roses, a riot of color that covered old stone walls and was barely held back from bursting across the path. Corbin didn't want to get too distracted. They were here for a reason, and he wanted to be useful to Luke. The man who'd led them out introduced them to Arthur Pennington. He'd blended in with the rest of the gardeners at first, but as soon as Corbin looked into his face, he'd seen differences. Definitely the owner of the house and not an employee. They were going to have a good time with this one. He dusted the dirt off of his hands onto well-worn trousers and shook their hands politely. Still looked pretty damn wary.

"LORD WELLESLEY?" Luke began. "We have a few questions about your friend, Thomas Hughes."

"He's not my friend. We were in a business arrangement. I haven't been close with Hughes in years."

"He was murdered two nights ago. We were hoping you might have some information that could help us."

"Why would I know anything about that?"

Here we go again. These people were like a permanent brick wall, every last one of them. Corbin didn't figure they'd get much out of Arthur Pennington, but they'd driven all the way up here so there was no point in giving up.

"We think you do. Miss Bixley, an associate of Thomas Hughes, said she'd heard you two arguing on the phone. That you'd had some sort of falling out."

"Are you asking me about his... *mistress*?" Pennington looked scandalized.

"We're asking you if you might know who had a grudge against him."

"Everyone," he said like it was a foregone conclusion. From what they'd learned so far, Hughes had definitely made his bed when it came to women, but they didn't know he'd had so many enemies.

Corbin was suddenly much more interested. "What do you mean by that?" he asked.

"Thomas wasn't the best business partner. It's not on to speak ill of the dead, so I'll leave his soul a rest, but I didn't wish to be business partners with him any longer. I think that should be enough to suffice."

"Did you have problems with him? Ones that might lead you to make a few phone calls?" Luke asked. He was pushing but that seemed to be the only thing that got a reaction.

"If you're asking me if I had Thomas Hughes killed, I'm telling you I've never been so insulted. I got far away from him and his *dealings* and stayed there. That argument his woman friend overheard was me telling him that I wasn't getting back in. If you ask me, the woman was in it up to her eyelids. And she wasn't the only one."

Helpful. They already knew that. They just couldn't prove it.

"What sort of dealings did Hughes have?" Luke asked him. "Were they illegal? Who are you implying was involved?"

Venerable Lord Wellesley snorted. "Well, it surely wasn't legal. Hughes was richer than most of us but he had no problems expanding on that wealth. He held a few well-connected positions in the financial community. He was quite ready to use them."

"To do what?"

Arthur looked at the house. "I think this conversation is about over. I don't have the details you're looking for. Only rumors."

"What are these rumors?"

"You might want to take a good look at his bank accounts. *All* of them. I think you'll find some discrepancies if what I've heard is correct. I know he kept his login information somewhere on that computer he was always carting around."

Secret bank accounts, peers who got far away from him, a shifty mistress, and a wife who couldn't stand the sight of him. Hughes was getting better by the moment.

"One final thing. You were on the roster for the North Yorkshire Riding Club Benefit for the night of August 15th. Is there confirmation you attended?"

"There will be pictures of the event all over the Internet. That should be confirmation enough for the likes of you."

"Yes. Thank you."

"Now, if that's all, I'd like to finish with my roses before I have my tea."

LUKE AND Corbin managed to find their way back to the car on their own.

"Hughes was a real dickhead, wasn't he? I'm starting to wonder why nobody killed him a long time ago," Corbin said when they got back into the car. He couldn't believe all the shit Hughes had gotten into. "What else can we find? It seems like this guy had no limit."

"But why?" Luke asked. "I still don't get why he's doing all of this. He was most likely doing some sort of money laundering, but he was richer than a king. He's got his mistress. And whoever else Pennington was referring to when he said 'she's not the only one.' Hughes is a total mystery."

"Was. Maybe it was that mystery that got him killed. When I... when I was studying him, I knew he wasn't exactly a stand-up guy. I never stole from people I wouldn't want to steal from, if you know what I mean, but he was *awful*. He was mean to his wife when he saw her. I didn't see the mistress since I was more interested in the main house and his schedule, but he was a jerk to his assistant. I should've figured he'd be in bad shit up to his asshole."

"Probably a lot farther." Luke rolled his eyes at the image. "It's like the more we dig, the more questions there are."

"I wonder if most people know how corrupt most of the upper crust is?"

Luke chuckled. "Not a popular opinion on these shores, mister."

"Nearly universally true, though. Believe me. I know."

Luke put his hand on Corbin's thigh. "It's a long drive back to London. Do you want to sleep for a while?"

"I'm not tired. And it was only a few hours. I know that's eternity here, but it's not so bad as far as I'm concerned. My family lives in Florida, remember?" Corbin found Luke's hand and threaded their fingers together. "It feels good to do this again," he said quietly. "I know I'm a mess you really don't want, but... I miss us."

"I don't get you," Luke said. "You keep saying stuff like that. I don't know what to think about it.

Corbin squeezed his hand. "I told you. I didn't fake anything with you. Nothing."

"You really had no idea what I did for a living when we met? That wasn't a setup?"

"Oh, lord no." Corbin nearly laughed at the absurdity. "The last thing in the world that would be good for me is being near someone like you, who's hunting me down. Like, if I'd been smart, I would've left the night you told me what you did and never looked back. But I couldn't. And look what happened."

"Why couldn't you?"

"I've *told* you. I loved you, Luke. I still do. I knew I should leave but I couldn't leave *you.* I guess you were my downfall after all. I thought you would be, and I was right."

Luke was quiet for a long time, but he kept his hand in Corbin's until he needed to shift, and then he put it back when he was done.

"I believe you," Luke said. "I couldn't stand to think you'd used me."

"I wouldn't. Ever. This whole thing was just…."

"A fucking mess?"

"Yeah," Corbin answered quietly. "But the best fucking mess I've ever been in."

CLARKE WAS in his office when Luke and Corbin got there that afternoon. He was on the phone, his face a study of bored efficiency. Luke still didn't like him or half of his detectives, but he wasn't about to get into that at the moment. They had work to do, and for the moment, they were working together. He and Corbin sat and waited for Clarke, who'd waved them in, to finish. When he hung up and looked at them expectantly, Luke started to talk.

"Corbin got into Hughes's laptop the other night," he said.

"How?" Clarke looked genuinely flabbergasted that a thief could manage what his tech guys had not.

"I'm good with computers." The same answer he'd given Luke. Luke figured there probably was a hell of a lot more to Corbin than he thought. He wondered if he'd ever get to find any of it out. The thought of that answer being no was really depressing.

"What did you find?" Clarke asked.

"A lot. Hughes wasn't a simple man. To start off with, he had a mistress. Letitia Bixley. She's not the easiest woman to talk to."

"You questioned her?" Clarke looked irritated. Luke conceded that it wasn't exactly in his official job description to question Clarke's suspects, just bring them to him.

"She gave us a name. Archer Pennington. Um, Lord Wellesley. We went to talk to him, as well."

"That's where you disappeared to? You just decided to go visit a *count* without asking?" Clarke's face had grown from irritated to a lovely eggplant color. Luke wasn't going to lie to himself. He was enjoying the director's outrage. He imagined his own director had a pissy phone call in his future. They *did* ask for his help.

"Viscount, I believe. And you asked for my help, Clarke. Now I'm helping. Pennington wasn't very open with us, but we did manage to get him to tell us he'd broken ties with Hughes, and that Hughes was involved in something he didn't approve of."

"What was Hughes involved in?"

"I'm guessing we're going to need a little more than questioning to get him to tell us. He acted like he didn't know, but that he figured it wasn't aboveboard. Bunch of bullshit, but I didn't have a warrant to search the premises."

"Did it occur to you I could've gotten one?"

"Because he'd been arguing with our victim? That's not enough for a warrant. Not anywhere I've worked."

"I've gotten one on less before. A lord was murdered, Mr. Eldridge. We need to produce answers, not vague hints and accusations."

"Corbin and I were going to go talk with Miss Bixley again today. There were some discrepancies between Hughes's bank balances and the balance in the accounting sheets his assistant gave us. Pennington told us to check that too. We are hoping that she's the answer somehow, but we need to know for sure."

"Don't lose your escort this time." Clarke gave Luke a pinched, sarcastic smile.

He said that like his men would've wanted to drive all the way to York with them. Luke figured he and Corbin had done them a favor. That had been a tiny bit satisfying as well. Luke wished he didn't like messing with Clarke's men as much as he did.

"You heard about that?" he asked.

"I don't like you, Interpol. You're starting to remind me why."

"I'd hold your dislike. If Corbin, er, Mr. Ford and I manage to crack this case, you'll probably want to change that to gratitude."

"Don't lose your escort when you speak to Miss Bixley next time," Clarke repeated.

"We won't. We're going to try to get a hold of her in the morning."

"I SWEAR to God, everything we find about our guy just gets worse and worse. Can't we declare it good riddance with the bastard and be done with the whole thing?" Corbin asked. He shoveled a huge bite of pad thai in his mouth. It had been such a long day. He was hungry and tired and just wanted to get back to Luke's apartment. He didn't know where he'd be sleeping. He'd spent the last two nights in Luke's bed, but it felt temporary. Like he was there because Luke hadn't noticed or something.

"Wouldn't that be nice and convenient? One not so great guy off the books. Unfortunately it doesn't exactly work that way."

"No kidding. Can I try some of your eggplant?"

"Aubergine, you mean."

Corbin rolled his eyes. "Can I try some of your *aubergine*?" Luke pushed his plate forward, and Corbin grabbed a slick chunk of eggplant in black bean sauce with his chopsticks. It was salty and fragrant, and squished pleasantly between his teeth. "I like this. Why didn't we ever come here before?"

Before. Before Corbin was a convict strapped to Luke's back, before he'd lost his trust, when the night would've ended with laughter, kisses, and a long shared shower before bed. He didn't know how many times he could think he wanted it back. The thought seemed to pop into his head every ten seconds or so. Probably wouldn't stop until Luke was far out of his life. Maybe not even then.

"I don't know. We were busy." Luke's lips quirked in a small smile, like he enjoyed remembering it as much as Corbin did. Even more surprising was when Luke stretched his feet out under the table and captured Corbin's between them. He was *flirting*. It felt almost right, like it had before.

For a while Corbin really did feel like he'd been flung backward in time, back to last week, to how perfect and wonderful everything had been before he'd royally fucked it up. They even stayed for coconut sticky rice and an extra drink before they grabbed a cab back to Luke's place.

"That was fun," Luke said in the back of the cab. "I didn't think we were going to do fun anymore."

"I didn't either, but I'm glad I was wrong," Corbin answered. He watched the rain patter on the windshield, drip down the windows, and gather in the crack where the glass disappeared into the door.

Luke reached across and curled his fingers around Corbin's hand, another surprise but an equally welcome one. "You staying in my room tonight?" he asked.

Corbin looked over. *Yes*, he wanted to say. *Tonight and every other night.* "You think it's a good idea?"

"Probably not. Do it anyway."

Luke squeezed Corbin's hand and threaded their fingers together. *Do it anyway.*

HOURS LATER, they lay in bed together in the dark, still sweaty, still breathing hard. Corbin had his arms wrapped around Luke. He couldn't quite believe it had happened again. It had been real and sweet and sexy. Luke still wasn't pulling away. Corbin trailed kisses up Luke's slick chest. He'd start all over again if he could. He wanted to touch every part of him to every part of Luke so he'd never forget.

"What are we going to do?" Luke finally said.

"What do you mean?" Corbin asked. He ran his fingers through Luke's hair and scratched gently at his scalp.

"I mean this. Us. You and me. What are we going to do?"

Corbin had felt it in his touch. Things were better between them, but he'd honestly not expected Luke to voice it. "I didn't think there was a you and me to do anything about. Is there?"

"I want there to be. No matter what my head says or my job, or, well, *laws*." Corbin chuckled softly. "This feels right. You and I feel right. It's crazy, but I can't get you out from under my skin. I don't think I want to anymore. I want us to be real."

"I do too. I always have."

"So what are we going to do?"

"I really don't know, babe. I wish I had answers. I do love you, though. A lot."

Luke breathed long and deep into Corbin's hair. "I love you too."

CHAPTER THIRTEEN

"MISS BIXLEY," Luke said.

She looked up as she locked the front door of her building. "Why are you here again? I thought I'd dealt with you lot already."

Theme of their life the past few days. Letitia Bixley looked even more nervous than she had the other day. Her hair was disheveled, and she'd replaced her heels and skirt with jeans and a pair of flats.

"We thought maybe you could help us again. We came across some new information when we were chatting with Lord Wellesley."

"Listen, I'm done with this," she said. "I've been the subject of some very nasty gossip in the right circles, and I had a very unique encounter the other night. Turns out I wasn't Thomas's only other woman. He wasn't going to marry me. He was stringing me along. I really don't have anything else to say to you. I don't care who killed the bastard. It wasn't me, but I wouldn't stand in their way if I had to do it all over again."

"Ma'am, we'd really like to not have to come back with a warrant. If everyone cooperates nicely, it'll be much more pleasant for everyone involved."

Letitia shot glances all around her, like she was looking for someone. "I'll talk later, okay?"

"Now would be a better time."

"Well, not for me. I have some errands to run and a life to live. I'll be home later. Near supper. You can come back then, and I'll answer any questions you want, although whatever you think I can tell you, I guarantee you it's not much."

"Five o'clock?" Luke asked.

"Five is fine."

With that, she scurried off, handbag tucked under her arm protectively, hair undone and blowing in the breeze.

"That was really odd," Corbin said.

"Yes. I agree."

THINGS WERE still odd when they returned later that evening. Quite a bit more odd, actually.

Letitia Bixley's building door was wide open. It wasn't a good sign. Luke wondered if she'd packed her shit, taken off, and gotten as far away from the investigation as she could in the few hours since they'd left her. He cursed himself for being a fool. He gestured for Corbin to get behind him and drew his gun.

"You need to stay out here," he whispered. Luke gestured at the two policemen to hang back.

"No," Corbin hissed back. "Are you out of your mind? I'm staying with you." He followed Luke into the posh building.

"Go outside."

"No."

They tiptoed up to the second level. Luke couldn't hear any noises from above, but the interior door was flung open as well and a trail of belongings had been strewn into the hallway. He picked up the pace, jogged up the last few stairs, and stopped at the open doorway to Letitia's flat. The place was a wreck, drawers pulled, curtains stripped from windows, and in the middle of it was Letitia. Luke gagged.

"Corbin, get back." he warned.

But it was too late. Corbin came around the corner. Luke felt it the moment he saw her. Gunshot wound to the head and one in the chest. She was more than dead, and whatever it was someone had come looking for, they sure as hell must've found it.

"Her laptop," Corbin muttered. "She had a laptop on that desk earlier. It's gone."

"What's with the laptops?" Luke whispered.

The desk was a wreck like everything else. Drawers pulled out, reams of papers littered the floor, photographs scattered on the ground. Luke walked over to the desk. He hoped there was a paper, maybe a notepad with indentations in it. Something. Instead he found piles of papers and old pictures. Nothing that seemed like it meant a thing to anyone but Letitia Bixley. He shuffled through them. They were old family pictures, Letitia at a younger age. And wait. Luke pried out one of the photos that was stuck in the seam of the drawer and stared at it for a moment before he realized that yes, he was seeing exactly what he thought he'd seen.

"What the hell...." He stared at the picture for a little longer, just to be absolutely sure.

That's him.

It was a long time ago, probably at least ten years, maybe more, but there was a teenaged *Morgan*. Morgan who worked for his office and had nothing to do with the Hughes case—or so Luke had thought. He at least had something to do with Letitia Bixley, which might have been the weirdest coincidence of all time. Or not. Morgan was in the old picture with Letitia's arm slung across his shoulders. She looked old enough to be a babysitter, maybe a friend. It was hard to tell. Morgan looked different too; laid-back where he'd become uptight, soft and smiley when he was usually very reserved. There was one thing that was very, very clear. It was him.

"Corbin, check this out. Morgan, *our* Morgan, knows Letitia Bixley."

"Doesn't he work for you? Why is there a picture of him with her?"

Luke was mystified. "I have no idea. And her computer's definitely gone." They didn't have time to ponder possible coincidences. "We need to get back to the apartment. *Now.*"

CHAPTER FOURTEEN

THEY TOLD their police tail to call in a homicide as they jogged out of Letitia Bixley's apartment.

"Where are you going?" one of them asked sharply.

"They took her computer," Luke said. "We have Hughes's laptop at my place. I need to get it before somebody else does."

"Go. We'll call this in." The officer waved them along. Luke and Corbin jogged to the waiting car.

"My apartment. Now," Luke said to the officer. Usually it was a pain in the ass to have them near. For the moment, it was better.

Luke's apartment was clean, empty of any strangers and obviously untouched. Whoever had been looking for Letitia's computer, whoever had killed her, wanted whatever information she had on there, but they didn't know enough to find Hughes's laptop as well. Corbin jogged into the room to check where he'd stored it, hidden inside a suitcase backed up against the back of Luke's closet, but it was still there.

"It's fine, Luke. I got it. The computer is safe."

Luke appeared in the doorway. "Hey, do you still have that comparison between Hughes' official schedule and that secondary one we found on his computer?"

"Yeah. Hold on. It's out in the living room with my stuff."

Luke winced like he remembered piling all of Corbin's stuff and hinting not very subtly that he wanted it gone. Corbin didn't really mind anymore. It was in the past. He and Luke were he and Luke again. Almost, at least. He made his way out to the living room and got the file that had the schedules' discrepancies highlighted. Like the night Hughes was supposed to have been in Birmingham for a meeting but was in London. The night he'd been shot.

159

"Here, look. These highlighted ones are the ones that are different. His assistant didn't have an answer for it. Only that Hughes didn't always require his presence."

"You think this is when Hughes was meeting whoever it was Pennington alluded to?" Luke asked.

"Yes. To do things with his 'financial connections.' Shit, could he have been more vague?" The whole thing was frustrating. Nobody knew anything, nobody was talking, they had two dead bodies and a bunch of walls thrown at them from every side. Corbin wondered if it was time to give everything they'd found to Scotland Yard and pull out. Judging by the determined look on Luke's face, that wasn't likely to happen.

"We might have to have Clarke go up there with a warrant." Luke didn't look happy about it. Exactly as Corbin assumed. "I don't know how sticky that can get, but if Pennington knows more, if he has any details and not just rumors, we really need that information. Because whoever Hughes was meeting with, he was supposed to meet during the exact window of his death."

"Whoever that was, Letitia knew something."

"And they silenced her before she could say anything more to us."

Luke crumpled the piece of paper in his hand angrily. "And what the hell does this have to do with Morgan?" He asked. "Why wouldn't he have told us he knew her?"

"Maybe nothing." That one, Corbin had no answer for. "You think we should talk to him?"

"Yeah. I'll call Waterman. Make sure he stays at the office. You up to it after what just happened?"

Corbin nodded. "I don't want to stay here alone."

"'Kay, babe. Let's go down to the office."

Babe. *Babe.* After dead bodies and old photographs and more weird facts unearthed it shouldn't have mattered. But it did.

IT FELT odd to be back in his office, like a million years had passed in the last day or so. Kelly gave him her usual brisk Kelly smile, Rob glanced at him with concern from where he was working on a document, and even Waterman seemed a little softer. Luke missed his team. He was tired of the never-ending downward spiral that was Hughes's life and probably death.

"You got Morgan for me?" he asked Waterman.

"He's in his office. I told him you wanted to speak to him."

Luke touched the photograph in his pocket. This wasn't going to be easy. "Full disclosure. I found a picture of Morgan with Letitia Bixley, Hughes's mistress. He knows her, and he didn't tell me. This might get a little... challenging."

"Why don't we take it into the conference room, then. I'll sit in."

Usually Luke hated when Waterman got involved in his day-to-day legwork. For once, he was intensely grateful. Luke went to move into the conference room. For a brief moment, he felt Corbin's hand at his back, just a tiny bit of comfort. He was grateful for that too.

The conference room was thick with tension of every kind. Luke, because he was about to start asking some really uncomfortable questions to a respected co-worker; Corbin probably because he didn't want to be there in general; and Morgan. Morgan had no idea what was coming but the second he walked in the room, he could probably tell it wasn't good.

Luke started by pulling the photograph out of his pocket and sliding it across the table to Morgan.

"Why didn't you tell us you knew her, Morgan? That's a pretty big detail to ignore."

Morgan turned a bright shade of pink. "I, um, hadn't seen her in years. I wasn't even sure it was the same person."

Luke looked at him for a long moment. *Good try, man. Not going to work.*

"She looks exactly the same, just a bit older. I recognized her immediately when I saw this picture. It took me a little bit longer to recognize you. Who was she to you?"

Morgan took his time to talk. He wrung his fingers together, bit his lip. He couldn't have been more obvious about his discomfort if he tried. "She was an au pair to my parents when I was younger. Mostly watched my little sister."

Luke knew Morgan came from a titled family. Somewhat wealthy but not by nobility standards—the poor relations in a circle of much more well-off landowners.

"And do you want to try telling us again why you didn't say that when she was in here the first time? Why *she* didn't say something?"

"I-I didn't think it was relevant to the case." Morgan shifted in his chair, understandably nervous. But that wasn't it. Morgan was the data guy, the one who wanted all the information. He knew one of Luke's suspects, had known her for years, and didn't think it seemed *relevant?* Something in Luke's brain clicked. *I call bullshit.*

"When was the last time you saw Miss Bixley?"

"When she was here. In the office."

He's lying.

"Before that. When had you seen her last?" Luke asked.

"A-At a reunion. I was about twenty."

Lying again. Luke would've thought that someone like Morgan, who did what they did for a living, would be better at telling a lie. Corbin pinched Luke's leg under the table. Luke nodded shortly to say he agreed.

Luke had an idea. "And you had no clue she was involved with Hughes?"

Morgan shook his head.

And here's where I get him. Luke watched carefully. "Do you know why someone would want to kill Letitia?"

Anyone else would've reacted. Shock. Sadness. Morgan didn't. Not for a few crucial seconds. Then he schooled his face into a mask of shock and said, "Letitia's dead?"

Got you. "Yes. This afternoon."

"Oh, God. I need to go call my mother. Can I call my mother?" Morgan looked at Waterman. He was good, better than Luke would've imagined, but it wasn't good enough. The bastard was lying. He'd killed Letitia himself. Luke just had to prove it.

"Are we done in here?" Waterman asked.

"I'm all done," Luke said.

Morgan surged out of his chair for the door.

"Watch him," Corbin said.

"I know."

MINUTES LATER, just as Luke expected after that interview, Morgan was bolting out of the offices. They didn't have anything on him other than Luke's intuition that he was lying. They needed him to *do* something. Looked like he was about to do it.

"Corbin. Come on. We're going to follow him."

Corbin nodded, and he and Luke walked out of the offices and turned in the direction that Morgan had gone. They rushed out into the fresh London air. The streets were teeming with people walking to lunch, going about their day. Morgan had disappeared into the crowd. How could he have done that? Morgan was nowhere near that slick. Luke searched the throng.

"Where is he? Shit, I don't see him," Luke said.

Corbin elbowed Luke. "Over there on the corner. He's heading into that bank."

"C'mon. Stay with me. At least ten feet behind him. Blend into the background. We want to see what he's doing, not spook him."

Corbin paused for a second and rolled his eyes. "Luke. I know how to follow someone."

Luke actually smiled this time. "I keep forgetting what you can do. Let's go."

They walked quickly across the intersection to the bank. It was big, stone, and imposing. Morgan had slipped inside. "What do you think he's doing in there?"

"We're going to find out," Luke said.

Turned out he was withdrawing cash. Lots of it. Morgan had a bag and was putting into it money the nervous-looking teller handed over to him. He was clearing out his accounts by the look of it. He was about to do something. He zipped up the bag, turned, and froze when he saw Luke and Corbin by the door. Morgan took off at a run for the exit on the other side of the bank.

"Shit. Run!"

The floor was slippery inside the bank, but when Luke pulled his badge out and held it up, the people moved out of their way. He and Corbin raced to the opposite door. Morgan was already out with his bag of cash. When they got outside, they looked right and left before they glimpsed him nearly a block away, trying to blend in with the crowd.

"There! There he is," Corbin said.

"This is gonna be impossible. We got to catch him before he gets to a Tube station, or we're completely screwed. He can lose us down there in a heartbeat."

Corbin and Luke threaded through the crowd, slipping between businessmen and women, tourists, and groups of children. Morgan was quick though; he turned a corner, heading toward the crowds near the abbey. The more people there were, the easier it would be for him to slip into the crowd. Luke knew it. Morgan knew it too.

"We have to run," Corbin said. "He's going toward Parliament. There are going to be about a million tourists once we get there."

Luke broke into a run, dodging people right and left, hoping Corbin was right behind him. They picked up the pace, drawing closer and closer until Morgan stopped right in front of them.

He turned and shouted. "Stop!" Morgan pulled out a gun and with no hesitation, fired at Luke. Point blank.

Tourists screamed and ducked down, and for a moment, everything froze. One of those surreal times when everything blurred but was super clear all at once.

Corbin leaped in front of Luke and pushed him to the ground. Luke's heart pounded in his chest. Morgan turned and started to run.

"You okay?" he asked Corbin.

"I'm fine. Go get him!"

Luke was a fast runner, but it turned out Corbin was faster. He didn't know that until Corbin overtook him and quickly closed the distance between them and Morgan. Morgan, who had a *gun*.

Shit. Pick up the pace.

The thought of Morgan firing another shot into the guy he loved was enough to nearly make him fall. Instead he ran as hard as he could, over grass and sidewalk, through throngs of panicked people. Corbin was still faster. Corbin leaped into the air and tackled Morgan. Morgan's gun and the bag of money went flying. Tourists who'd been waiting outside Westminster Abbey stared. Some snapped pictures. Luke rushed to help Corbin subdue Morgan. He grabbed both his wrists and held on.

"Don't move, dickhead. I can't believe I trusted you as part of my team, and you tried to kill me." Luke could barely breathe enough to get the sentence out, but he yanked hard enough to make Morgan wince. Felt good making the asshole hurt. He figured he'd better let off, though. Huge crowd around them and all. He dug his elbow into Morgan's spine and made him stop resisting.

"Fuck off, Eldridge," Morgan spat. "You don't know anything about me. Never even bothered to try. Superhero agent wouldn't know what it's always like to be not good enough. I wanted to be *something*."

"A murderer? Is that what you wanted to be?"

Morgan didn't answer. Luke pulled him off the ground and into a tight hold.

"Why'd you do it, Morgan? Why'd you kill Hughes? I know you didn't have this planned. The murder was sloppy. Look at what happened today. None of this was what you wanted. Why'd you do it?"

Luke's shoulder ached from where he'd tumbled to the ground, and his legs felt like lead. He dragged Morgan across the grass to the waiting Scotland Yard cars. It hadn't taken them long to catch up to Luke and Corbin. For once he was glad for their backup. They pulled Morgan away from him and pushed him into the car.

"He screwed me over," Morgan said. "He was going to turn me in. I was fucked either way."

"Turn you in for what? What did you and he do?"

Morgan laughed coldly. "Why the bloody hell do you think I'd tell you that? I'm sure you'll hear eventually, anyway. Everyone will." Then he smiled and sank down into the police car without another word.

CHAPTER FIFTEEN

IT WAS raining when they got back to the apartment, like somehow the sky knew what had gone down and was trying to rinse everything clean. Or else it was England. A quick dash through the rain and into the stairwell nearly soaked them through. Corbin wondered if this is what Luke always felt at the end of a case, this thrumming desperate need to release, the visceral thrill that raced over his skin. He wanted everything and nothing and too much all at once. The painful hours spent waiting while everything was settled, Morgan dealt with, things were put right, had stretched him thin until he barely felt like he could keep from exploding.

Corbin couldn't believe it was all about money. Well, he could. In a way, that was what his world had always been about too, but after he met Luke and realized there were other things, things that were more important, it was almost as if he couldn't see the other side of the fence anymore. Morgan had made a virus, simple as that. It had taken hours for Luke to drag it out of him bit by bit. The virus would've attached itself onto a server in the main London branch of the Bank of England and siphoned small amounts off of every transaction into an account Morgan had planned to share with Hughes, who was his only way into the private areas of the bank. Of course, Letitia had been his connection to Hughes.

According to Morgan, Hughes had gotten cold feet and pulled out at the last minute. Morgan had killed him, and then Letitia when she'd spooked. He had to be crazy. That was the only explanation. He wanted to feel like he was equal with the people he'd been surrounded by his whole life, and he'd killed two people because of it. Corbin still shuddered when he thought of how close Luke had been to becoming the third.

"You okay?" Luke asked as he let them both into the apartment.

"No. *Fuck,* how do you stand it?" Corbin asked. He thought he knew thrills, he thought he'd lived danger, but he'd never felt like he did right at that moment. "I feel. Shit. I don't even know. I feel like I'm going to combust."

"Adrenaline. You're not used to it."

"I don't know. Not like this. I thought I knew everything there is to know about adrenaline. Turns out that getting shot at isn't quite the same as stealing a necklace."

Luke wrapped his arms around Corbin and squeezed. "What you did out there for me. You're amazing. I could've died."

"I... had to. The thought of you dying like that. I couldn't stand it." Corbin dragged off his wet shirt and shivered in the darkness of the apartment. "Can you please? I need to touch your skin. I need you."

"Yes." Luke pulled his shirt off and then wrapped Corbin in his arms. "You're freezing. Let's get in the shower. Warm you up."

"Don't want a shower. Want you."

Luke pulled back and looked at him, rubbed his hands up and down Corbin's arms. He must've seen the desperation written on his face, because he nodded.

"Yeah, fuck. Of course."

Corbin dragged Luke into the room, but Luke was the one who pulled Corbin onto the bed. Stripped off his shoes, his pants, until he was naked and wanting and ready. Luke made quick work of his own clothes. Corbin had longed for his muscles and lean hips. It was a relief to be able to look his fill. He needed to touch. Corbin opened his arms for Luke, pulled him in. Wrapped his legs around Luke.

"Don't go slow. I need this tonight."

Luke nodded like he understood everything Corbin couldn't say. He simply reached into his drawer and slicked his fingers up, sinking one, then two inside. It felt like heaven and perfect and not enough. Corbin wanted more than teasing, aching fingers. He wanted everything.

"Fuck. Please."

Luke fumbled with a condom and dragged it on. He slicked his length and lined it up. "You sure you're ready?"

"Yes. Now."

Corbin grasped his hips with sweaty hands and pulled as much as he could, trying to show Luke what he needed and wanted.

Luke slowly pushed in, groaning, until he was in to the hilt. Corbin loved the feeling of Luke so deep in him.

"You feel so damn good," Luke growled. "The best. Every time."

Corbin didn't want it to end, not when he and Luke could very well be over in the morning, but he wanted to feel everything he could feel. As hard as he could feel it. Maybe that way he could remember. "Move. Please."

"I won't last if I do it that way. I'm too wound up."

"It's okay. I won't either. We have all night."

Luke rolled his hips, slowly at first, then harder and deeper until Corbin felt it in his teeth, just the way he needed it. "I love this so much," he breathed. "Love you. Babe. *Fuck.*"

Luke shuddered and bit his neck. It was sure to leave marks. Corbin wanted to be marked so he'd never forget. They moaned and arched, and Corbin's cock rubbed on the slick skin of Luke's belly.

It was too much. All the feeling and want and need and worry from earlier. Corbin had a hard time breathing. He could barely see, let alone think enough to do anything but grasp Luke and try to get him closer. Corbin needed to be closer. He wanted to breathe Luke in and taste and touch and never forget.

Corbin wrapped his legs around Luke's hips. "So close," he breathed. "I need it."

"Me too. I'm—" Luke breathed hard and bit down on Corbin's neck even harder. He pummeled his hips in, once, twice, three more times, until Corbin was shuddering and coming all over both of them. Luke didn't last more than another stroke before he followed.

After that they dragged themselves into the shower. It was relaxing to stand under the water with Luke. Just gentle touches and kisses. Sometimes Corbin thought he'd missed this part even more than the sex.

"I love you," he whispered into Luke's chest. "I know I've caused you so much trouble, but I'm glad we met."

"Me too. Whatever I said to you the past couple of days, I'm never going to be sorry for that."

Corbin's throat felt thick. He didn't want it to end but end it would. No matter what the outcome was in the morning, no matter what was said, he couldn't see a future for him and Luke. Corbin sighed and pressed one more kiss to Luke's wet chest.

"I'm gonna get out. You want some tea?"

"Sure. I'll have some tea."

"HEY, BABE. Don't look so defeated."

They were in bed, showered, clean, with sleep pants on. Corbin's stomach, which had churned with adrenaline, filled with heavy dread. "You're not the one going on trial in the near future. The case is over. They're taking me in tomorrow, to wherever it is Waterman wants to send me. I don't know how I'm going to face that, babe. I'm terrified."

"It might not be that bad. You could get a really good deal. You helped catch Morgan. You saved my life. They're not going to look at that and not consider it."

"I know. I'm just scared. I can't be locked up like that."

"We'll make it work somehow, okay? We'll make it work."

Corbin nodded and pushed into Luke, nuzzling back for what could be the last bit of Luke's skin he'd feel in a long, long time.

"You wanna just go to sleep?" Luke asked.

"Yes. No. I'm not sure. I want to lie here with you and be quiet. Be together."

"I can do that," Luke said. He pulled Corbin tighter in the darkness and pressed kisses to the back of his neck. Corbin thought he might have heard the word "love" and even "forever," little whispers mixed in with the kisses, but he couldn't be sure. Eventually, he closed his eyes and fell asleep.

"MORNING," CORBIN said. He leaned over Luke and smooshed their lips together.

Luke laughed and grabbed Corbin, rolling them over in bed. He didn't know what the day would bring, the future, Corbin's trial, any of it. He just knew he was still in love, and if nothing else worked out, at least that felt good for as long as it lasted. He kissed Corbin again, tangled his fingers in sandy hair, and tried to get his fill of Corbin's smell and the way he sounded when he laughed into Luke's neck. He knew it wasn't possible. He would never be able to get his fill. Corbin had wormed his way in until he was part of Luke, and even when Luke was so angry he wanted to throw up and shoot things, Corbin was still in him in every way. He probably always would be.

"I'm gonna miss you," Luke said. "You…. Fuck, I don't even know how to say this. I really hope things go well for you, and it's not too long. I want you to find me, okay?"

"Really? No matter what?"

The look Corbin gave Luke was weird. Pensive. Sad. Luke supposed he had a right to feel those things. He was about to get turned in to any number of authorities to await a hearing and trial. Who knew how effective Scotland Yard's recommendation would be? Things were about to get weird for him. For both of them, because there was no way Luke wasn't going to be there to watch.

"Yes. Really. I want you to find me when all of this is over. I *love* you. It might be crazy with what you did and what I still do, but I love you. I don't see that changing ever. Did you really mean you were done?"

"If I got to be with you? Yes, I meant it."

"Then I'll be waiting for you."

"Okay," Corbin kissed him. "I'm going to find you. I'll always find you."

"Good." It was weird and serious, and Luke meant every damn word of it. He'd waited until he was thirty-eight years old to find the guy he wanted to spend the rest of his damn life with. He could wait some more. Corbin rolled over and looked at the clock. "It's later than I thought it was."

"We still have a few hours," Luke said. "It's early." He planned to spend them in bed, where he and Corbin belonged.

Corbin cupped his face. He looked awfully sad. It was too early to be sad. Not yet. Not until it was time for them to go back to the office and Corbin turned himself in. "I love you so much," he whispered. "You've changed my whole life."

"I love you too," Luke said. "I always will."

"I'm so sorry. You have to understand. I love you."

"Sorry fo—" Luke felt a prick on the side of his neck. A needle, sharp and tiny. It only took seconds for the world to go black.

WHEN LUKE woke up, it was clearly hours later. The sky had darkened, and he had a raging headache. He heard noises in the living room and wandered out, feeling drunk and woozy, to find half his unit and a few policemen standing in his living room.

"What happened?" he asked.

"The alarm went off on his anklet. Scotland Yard was here in minutes, but he got away. They never even saw him." Kelly looked at him kindly. "He probably could've gotten away at any time, Luke. He waited until the case was solved."

"How long have you guys been here?"

"Hours. You were drugged, but you weren't in any danger. We let you sleep it off."

There had been officers in his apartment all *day,* and he'd slept right through the whole damn thing? "Where's Morgan?"

"Morgan?" Kelly asked. "He's not our problem anymore. They have him." She hooked a thumb at the policemen.

"Did he say anything to you?" Rob asked.

"Corbin?"

"Man, you're still drugged. Yes, Corbin."

Luke thought about that morning. It seemed like he had to wade through hours in his brain, fuzzy underwater moments that didn't quite clear up. Finally, he remembered. "He apologized. Said I'd have to understand."

"So that's it, then. He's gone."

"Yeah," Luke said quietly, trying to talk and think and exist over the pounding pain in his chest. "Corbin's gone."

Luke was pretty sure he'd never see him again.

Four months later….

LUKE TURNED off his computer and went to lock his office up. It had been dark for at least an hour if he'd counted right. He hadn't really been looking out the window. There wasn't much to see. Just the same buildings and cars and streets he always saw, dark and wet and tired in the impending winter.

It was December. The world was lit up with the beginnings of the holiday season, but Luke, who rarely got excited for the holidays, had made a competitive sport out of ignoring the whole damn thing. Everything was still gray to him. Months later, and he still smelled Corbin sometimes when he found a shirt in his closet, still thought he heard his laugh sometimes on the Tube.

So yeah, Luke wasn't exactly in the Christmas spirit. If he could spend the holiday with a pizza and some soccer on the television and sleep the rest of it away, he'd do that in a heartbeat. That wasn't what other people had in mind for him. He was planning to spend the day at Rob and Trish's house. It was pretty much mandatory. They were still treating him like he was fragile. He supposed he was. It had taken a lot of effort to pull himself up by the ass and keep going after what had happened in August.

MOST OF the team was gone. Kelly had traveled to Sheffield for the week to spend it up north with her family. Rob was shopping for the girls while Trish made dinner. Even Waterman's office was dark. Leslie, who'd replaced Morgan, was working at her desk, probably still trying to prove she belonged, that they'd made the right choice bringing her from the Manchester office after the disaster that was Morgan. She was smart and interesting and a better fit after a few months than Morgan had been after years with the team.

"Hey, Leslie. You heading home anytime soon?" Luke called.

She looked up with a smile. "Yes. I just wanted to finish these last few reports, then I'm going to head out for some dinner with my husband. Do you have any plans this weekend?"

Sit in front of the television and think about sand and palm trees and a kiss he'd never feel again. He had to get gifts for Rob and Trish and the girls, but other than that, he was going back to his competitive avoidance tactics. And moping. That was another sport he'd gotten to be world-class at. Probably why Rob and Trish treated him like he was about to break into a million pieces. Sometimes, it felt like he was. He didn't know it was possible to miss one person *so* much. He went back and forth between wishing the feelings would just go away and Corbin, wherever the hell he was, would show up on his doorstep some night with the key he still had. Just so Luke would know where he was. And maybe touch him again.

"Not really doing much. Probably just veg in front of the telly unless Waterman needs me for something."

He'd said *telly*. Time to move back to America.

LUKE HAD been thinking about it a lot lately. Asking for a transfer to somewhere warm like Miami or Hawaii or Brazil. Hopping on a plane. He wanted a change of pace, needed it even. It had been so long since he'd done anything but trudge around London, wishing he were anywhere else. It would be weird to leave Rob. They'd been together since the dawn of time. But the girls were happy in their school, and Rob was happy in their office, and he'd never ask them to follow, even if they offered. Luke hadn't made any real effort to find a new assignment anyway, as much as he knew he needed to get the hell out.

Maybe after the holidays.

Luke waved one more time at Leslie, then went out into the biting cold. It would be worse in January and February. It always was. The wet winter chill had returned to England, and it would last for months. Luke wasn't looking forward to it. There wasn't anyone to warm him from the wet and rain.

He thought about stopping by the pub for a drink. Maybe find someone with zero commitment potential to bring home for a night. He hadn't been able to bring himself to do that yet, either. That was right on his list after looking into a transfer. Again, maybe after the holidays.

He trudged to the Tube stop and down the stairs, holding his scarf against him so the violent updrafts didn't whip it off. The trains were packed, even though it was after rush hour, and he was glad to be off it. It was good to be nearly home even if home didn't quite feel the same anymore.

It wasn't a long walk from to his building, but it wasn't a pleasant one either. The streets were crowded with people laughing and talking, planning upcoming holiday fun, hands cupped around lattes and hot cocoas in festive paper cups. Luke had to hold back the instinct to knock the cups out of people's hands. Ask them how they dared to be so very happy when he was so miserable.

I definitely need a change of scene.

HIS LIVING room light was on. He noticed it from the street. Luke was fairly sure he'd turned it off when he left that morning in the pale early morning light. He'd turned it off the night before, in fact, and hadn't turned it back on. How could it possibly be…. He got an uneasy feeling in his belly, a little nervous and fluttery at the same time. He was on edge as he withdrew his key and opened the front door of the building. He was still on edge as he walked up to his second-floor apartment and opened the locked door.

On first appearance, everything was just as he'd left it. His blanket was strewn across the couch, the remote was balanced on the arm, his slippers were sitting in the hallway outside his bathroom. And then he saw it. There was a package on his coffee table, gift wrapped for Christmas, with two things sitting on top: an antique pocket watch and a square of paper.

Luke's heart sped until he felt every thump pound in his throat. Corbin. Corbin had been here. He lifted the watch and held it in his hand. It couldn't be cheap; it was heavy and intricate, old, made out of some sort of copper with inlaid stone. The watch was beautiful, but that wasn't what made Luke's throat get thick and tight. It wasn't what made his fingers tremble.

There was a note, small and square, on the same thick linen paper as the rest. Luke doubted it would be poetry and more clues, and it wasn't. There were four, short handwritten words.

I still love you.—C.

Corbin was still out there, watching him, waiting for the right time to come back to him.

And Luke wasn't going anywhere.

M.J. O'SHEA grew up and still lives in sunny Washington State, and while she loves to visit other places, she can't imagine calling anywhere else home. M.J. spent her childhood writing stories. Sometime in her early teens, the stories turned to romance. Most of those stories were about her, her friends, and their favorite cute TV stars. She hopes she's come a long way since then....

When M.J.'s not writing, she loves to play the piano and cook and paint pictures, and, of course, read. She likes sparkly girly girl things, owns at least twenty different-colored headbands, and she has two dogs who sit with her when she writes. Sometimes her dog comes up with the best ideas for stories... when she's not busy napping.

E-mail: mjosheaseattle@gmail.com
Website: http://www.mjoshearomance.com
Blogs: http://mjoshea.com/ and http://mjandpiper.blogspot.com
Twitter: @MjOsheaSeattle

Catch My Breath

By M.J. O'Shea

Danny Bright was born to entertain. He just needs his big break. So when he hears that Blue Horizon Records is holding auditions looking for the next big thing, Danny jumps at the chance. It doesn't turn out exactly as he imagined, though. Instead of getting solo contracts, Danny and four other guys are put into a boy band.

Innocent, idealistic Elliot Price thinks he's headed for college. An impulsive decision to sing in the local talent search changes all that. A bigwig producer happens to see him, hands him a business card, and turns Elliot's life upside down.

Elliot and Danny are close from the beginning. They love all the guys, but it's different with each other. Soon their friendship turns into feelings more intense than either of them can ignore. The other three boys only want Danny and Elliot to be happy, but when their management team and record label discover two of their biggest tween heartthrobs are in a relationship, they're less than pleased. Danny and Elliot find themselves in the middle of a circle of lies and cover-ups, all with one bottom line—money. They have to stay strong and stick together if they don't want to lose themselves… and each other.

Corkscrewed

By M.J. O'Shea

CORKSCREWED
M.J. O'SHEA

Cary Talbot has found the perfect mark. Marigold Shelley is filthy rich, and her newly found grandson, Isaac Shelley, is poised to inherit her huge estate, complete with a priceless wine collection. Cary concocts a plan to con both of them into selling the crown jewel of that collection to him at a bargain price. Since Isaac is young, single, and gay, part of Cary's scheme to get close to the Shelleys includes seduction.

But Isaac isn't the sheep he appears to be. He isn't even the grandson he appears to be. Isaac is, in fact, running quite the con of his own.

These two masters of the confidence game are pitted against each other, and both are after the ultimate prize—a chunk of the huge Shelley fortune. It's only when a third cunning player comes in and is ready to outwit them both that they must band together and beat their opponent or see all they've worked for slip from their grasp one ruby-red drop at a time.

http://www.dreamspinnerpress.com

Newton's Laws of Attraction

By M.J. O'Shea

Rory was Ben's oldest and best friend until senior year of high school, when they confessed they'd harbored feelings for each other all along. They enjoyed only a few months of happiness until Ben chose closeted popularity over true love… and he's regretted it ever since.

Eight years later, Ben is out and proud and teaching art at the same high school he graduated from. When he learns the chemistry teacher is retiring, he's excited to meet her replacement until he finds out the brand new teacher is none other than Rory Newton—the first love he's never quite gotten over. Despite a painfully awkward start, it doesn't take Ben long to realize he'll do whatever it takes to win Rory back. But it's starting to look like even his best might not be enough.

http://www.dreamspinnerpress.com

Impractical Magic

By M.J. O'Shea

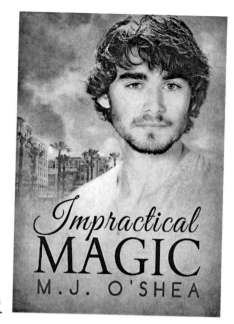

Physics teacher Fenton Keene is looking forward to a summer of doing nothing but hanging out with friends and maybe getting into a little trouble. With his best friend out of town, trouble seems like the best option and it comes in the form of his building's newest temporary resident, a gorgeous fireman named Kevin.

Fen's been attracted to men before, but this is the first time he's considered acting on it. And act he does.

Fen and Kevin have an intense summer fling. Just in time for Kevin to go home, more feelings develop than Fen can ignore, but they don't stop Kevin from leaving. Once Kevin's gone, Fen can't stop thinking about him. That's when reality sets in and Fen faces the difficulties of distance and fidelity, while Kevin balks at Fen's reluctance to tell his friends and family. They just need to find a way to make their magic more practical.

http://www.dreamspinnerpress.com

Coming Home

Rock Bay: Book One

By M.J. O'Shea

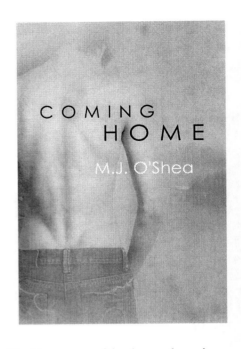

Tallis Carrington ruled Rock Bay with his gang of jocks and an iron fist—until a scandal destroyed his family's name. Ten years later Tallis is dead broke, newly homeless, and on the walk of shame to end all walks of shame. He needs money and needs it fast, and Rock Bay is the only home he knows. But the people of Rock Bay haven't forgotten him—or the spoiled brat he used to be.

The only person in town willing to overlook his past is Lex, the new coffee shop owner, who offers Tally a job even though he appears to despise Tally based on his reputation alone. When Tally discovers his gorgeous boss is the kid he tortured back in high school, Lex's hot and cold routine finally makes sense. Now Tally has to pull out all the stops to prove he was never really the jerk he seemed to be. After all, if he can win Lex's heart, the rest of the town should be a piece of coffee cake.

http://www.dreamspinnerpress.com

Letting Go

Rock Bay: Book Two

By M.J. O'Shea

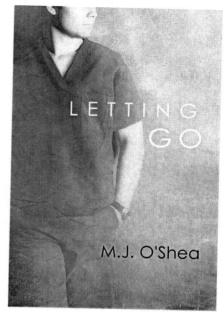

Drew McAuliffe has lived in the small town of Rock Bay most of his adult life. He'd like to be happy, but not at the cost of having his private life under his nosy neighbors' microscope, so he keeps his bisexuality under wraps.

After a messy breakup that caused him to pack up and move to Astoria, on the Oregon coast, Mason Anderson decides to avoid drama of the romantic kind. All he wants is to start over—alone.

But Drew and Mason were meant to meet. The long looks and awkward half hellos chance offered were never going to be enough. But when they do finally come together on the worst night possible, misconceptions and problems from their pasts get in the way. Until Mason learns to trust again—and until Drew learns to let go of who he thinks he is—a real connection is nothing but a pipe dream.

http://www.dreamspinnerpress.com

Finding Shelter

Rock Bay: Book Three

By M.J. O'Shea

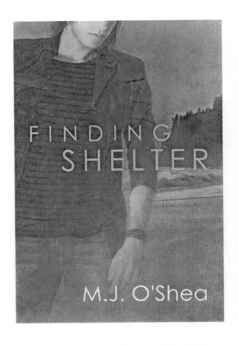

Justin Foster has nineteen years of nothing but trouble behind him. After escaping his abusive father, he finds himself in Rock Bay, Washington, with his cousin Travis. Justin is bruised and has a hard time trusting, but with the help of his family and the small town, he might be able to heal.

Logan O'Brien is also new in town, hoping he can finally get away from his past and the memories of the girlfriend who shattered his heart. It doesn't take him long to realize Rock Bay can be more than safe harbor: it can also be home. And for the first time in his life, he finds himself captivated by a man—by Justin.

Justin is attracted to Logan too, but he's also wary. Physically, Logan reminds him a bit too much of the closeted jerks who used to beat him up after school. But after one awkwardly amazing kiss, he's smitten, despite how his past and insecurities continue to haunt him. Logan's love, faith, and stubbornness are just what Justin needs to believe their love is worth fighting for.

http://www.dreamspinnerpress.com

Macarons at Midnight

A Just Desserts Novel

By M.J. O'Shea & Anna Martin

Tristan Green left his small English town for Manhattan and a job at a high profile ad agency, but can't seem to find his bearings. He spends a lot of time working late at night, eating and sleeping alone, and even more time meandering around his neighborhood staring into the darkened windows of shops. One night when he's feeling really low, he wanders by a beautiful little bakery with the lights still on. The baker invites him in, and some time during that night Tristan realizes it's the first time he's really smiled in months.

Henry Livingston has always been the odd duck, the black sheep, the baker in an old money family where pedigree is everything and quirky personalities are hidden behind dry martinis and thick upper east side townhouse facades. Henry is drawn to Tristan's easy country charm, dry English wit, and everything that is so different from Henry's world.

Their new romance is all buttercream frosting and sugared violets until Tristan's need to fit in at work makes him do something he desperately wishes he could undo. Tristan has to prove to Henry that he can be trusted again before they can indulge in the sweet stuff they're both craving.

http://www.dreamspinnerpress.com

Soufflés at Sunrise

A Just Desserts Novel

By M.J. O'Shea & Anna Martin

"Welcome to a new season of *Burned*, where we find fresh new cooking talent… and a few culinary disasters! Every season we do something a little different, and this time it's all about the sweet things in life. Get ready in week one as twenty pastry chef hopefuls and dessert connoisseurs compete for the thirteen coveted workspaces in our *Burned* kitchen. With stakes this big, we ask the one question on everyone's mind: Do these chefs have what it takes to rise to the top? Or will they get *Burned*?"

Burned contestants Chase and Kai are attracted from the start and can't wait to spend more time getting to know each other… until they see the first episode treatment and realize the producers intend to portray them as bitter enemies. At first it's fun to pretend to bicker—enemies on film, lovers when the cameras stop rolling—but soon it's hard not to take the faux rivalry seriously. It's only when their choice is to band together and bake their way to the final or get burned that they find where their real loyalties lie.

http://www.dreamspinnerpress.com

Moonlight Becomes You

Lucky Moon: Book One

By M.J. O'Shea & Piper Vaughn

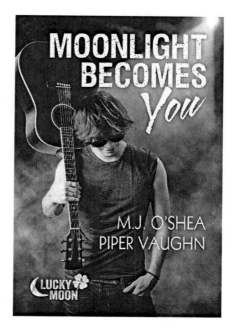

Eleven years ago, Shane Ventura made the biggest mistake of his life when he caved in to pressure from his record label to kick his best friend, Jesse Seider, out of their band, Luck. To this day, Shane has never wanted anyone more, and all the sex and alcohol in the world can't fill the void Jesse left behind. Not even the prospect of teaming up with Britain's hottest band, Moonlight, for a massive world tour can get him out of his funk. Then he meets lead singer Kayden Berlin and falls into instant lust.

Kayden may act like he's not interested, but Shane knows he feels the spark between them. Yet the harder Shane pushes, the more Kayden pulls away, until one explosive night leaves Shane with a broken heart. That seems to be his lot—lucky at everything but love. Shane still has one lesson left to learn, though: when it comes to love, you can't always leave things to chance.

http://www.dreamspinnerpress.com

The Luckiest

Lucky Moon: Book Two

By M.J. O'Shea & Piper Vaughn

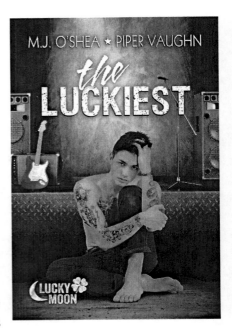

Rock star Nick Ventura has finally hit rock bottom. Jealous of his brother's new love, he overindulges in his usual vices and winds up crashing his car into a department store in a drunken haze. Publicly humiliated and on the verge of jail time, he enters a court-ordered rehabilitation program.

Nutritionist Luka Novak is flamboyant, effeminate, and the type of gay man bisexual Nick would normally sneer at. But Luka's sunny nature hides a deep hurt caused by an unfaithful ex-boyfriend. As much as Luka knows he should be wary of Nick's reputation, he's drawn to Nick despite himself. Their tentative friendship turns into romance, but Luka soon comes to realize Nick's fear of losing his bad boy reputation means he'll probably never go public with their relationship.

Nick never needed anyone until Luka came into his life. Now he has to reconcile his carefree past with the future he suddenly wants more than anything. And the first lesson he must learn is how to become the man both he and Luka need him to be, rather than stay the boy he always was. Alone.

http://www.dreamspinnerpress.com

One Small Thing

One Thing: Book One

By Piper Vaughn & M.J. O'Shea

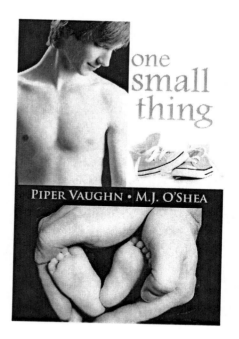

"Daddy" is not a title Rue Murray wanted, but he never thought he'd have sex with a woman either. Now he's the unwitting father of a newborn named Alice. Between bartending and cosmetology school, Rue doesn't have time for babies, but he can't give her up. What Rue needs is a babysitter, and he's running out of options. He's on the verge of quitting school to watch Alice himself when he remembers his reclusive new neighbor, Erik.

Erik Van Nuys is a sci-fi novelist with anxiety issues to spare. He doesn't like people in general, and he likes babies even less. Still, with his royalties dwindling, he could use the extra cash. Reluctantly, he takes on the role of manny—and even more reluctantly, he finds himself falling for Alice and her flamboyant father.

Rue and Erik are as different as two people can be, and Alice is the unlikeliest of babies, but Rue has never been happier than when Alice and Erik are by his side. At least, not until he receives an offer that puts all his dreams within reach and he's forced to choose: the future he's always wanted, or the family he thought he never did.

http://www.dreamspinnerpress.com

One True Thing

One Thing: Book Two

By Piper Vaughn & M.J. O'Shea

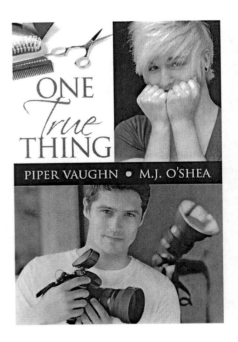

Dustin Davis spent years wishing for a prince but kissing frog after slimy frog. When he sees Archer Kyriakides for the first time, Dusty thinks his luck has finally changed. Archer could be it. The One. But their hot and cold romance leaves Dusty confused: why does it feel right one moment and wrong the next? It doesn't make sense—until the day Dusty meets Archer's identical twin, Asher, and realizes he's been seeing them both.

Asher Kyriakides dreams of being a fashion photographer, but he's stuck with a job he hates and an irresponsible playboy brother whose habits drive him absolutely insane, especially when he finds out Archer is dating the cute little blond Asher can't seem to forget. Torn between loyalty and desire, Asher does nothing but try to warn Dusty away.

But when Archer finally goes too far, Dusty turns to Asher for comfort, and Asher knows he can't refuse. It isn't long before they realize they're falling fast, but more than one thing stands in their way, not the least of which is Archer, who isn't quite ready to stop being a thorn in his brother's side.

http://www.dreamspinnerpress.com

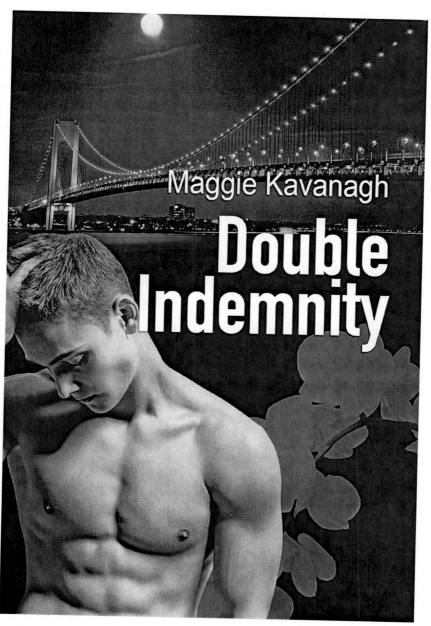

Maggie Kavanagh

Double Indemnity

http://www.dreamspinnerpress.com

Amy Lane

Candy
MAN

http://www.dreamspinnerpress.com

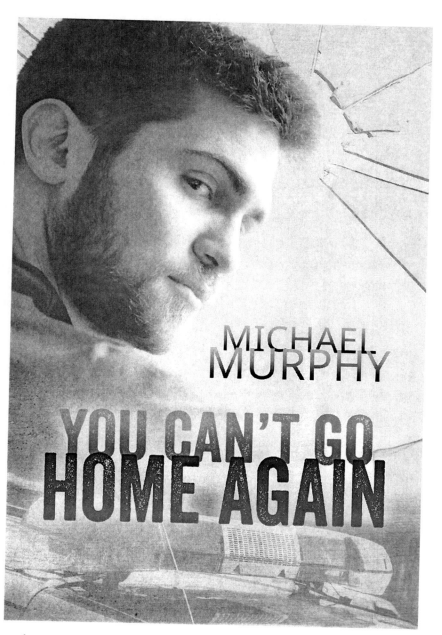

MICHAEL MURPHY

YOU CAN'T GO HOME AGAIN

http://www.dreamspinnerpress.com

CPSIA information can be obtained at www.ICGtesting.com
Printed in the USA
LVOW10s0230140916

504503LV00013B/294/P